A ROPE FOR IRON EYES

Notorious bounty hunter Iron Eyes corners the deadly Brand brothers in the house with the red lamp above its door. As the outlaws enjoy themselves, Iron Eyes bursts in with guns blazing. But Matt Brand and his siblings are harder to kill than most wanted men: they fight like tigers, and Iron Eyes is lynched before they ride off. Yet even a rope cannot stop Iron Eyes. And he is determined to resume his deadly hunt, regardless of whoever dares stand in his way.

RORY BLACK

A ROPE FOR IRON EYES

Complete and Unabridged

LINFORD
Leicester

First published in Great Britain in 2013 by
Robert Hale Limited
London

First Linford Edition
published 2016
by arrangement with
Robert Hale Limited
London

A catalogue record for this book is available
from the British Library.

ISBN 978–1–4448–2678–4

Published by
F. A. Thorpe (Publishing)
Anstey, Leicestershire

Set by Words & Graphics Ltd.
Anstey, Leicestershire
Printed and bound in Great Britain by
T. J. International Ltd., Padstow, Cornwall

This book is printed on acid-free paper

Dedicated to
Eileen Gunn with thanks

Prologue

The streets of Anvil City glowed with the amber illumination of countless coal tar lanterns as the tall figure of the bounty hunter strode out from the hotel lobby. He paused just long enough to pull a cigar from his deep bullet-filled trail-coat pocket and crush a cockroach under his boot heel. Iron Eyes ran a match down a wooden upright and studied the street carefully as his bony hands cupped its flame to the cigar gripped between his teeth. He sucked in the acrid smoke, then tossed the match away. The evening breeze extinguished the blackened match long before it hit the sand.

A long trail of smoke drifted from his scarred lips as Iron Eyes surveyed the length of the town's main street. His eyes narrowed.

Something was gnawing at the craw of the skeletal hunter of men. Something

1

was wrong. For some irrational reason the emaciated figure was troubled by this seemingly peaceful town. On the face of it Anvil City appeared to be the most tranquil place he had found himself in for years.

Yet he did not believe it.

Iron Eyes inhaled the cigar smoke deeply. As it drifted from between his razor-sharp teeth his bullet-coloured eyes searched every shadow for the trouble that he sensed was brewing somewhere amongst the seemingly peaceful community. Not even graveyards were this peaceful, he thought.

He sensed impending danger, yet there was no sign of it wherever he looked. It was as though the Grim Reaper was whispering into his ear, warning him that soon it would be his turn to die. The evening breeze blew his mane of long black hair off his face, revealing his scarred features. But there was no one to see the mutilated face. The street was empty, except a few horses tied to hitching rails.

Deathly silence prevailed.

Iron Eyes wondered if that was the reason why he felt so uneasy. He was not used to such peaceful surroundings. Even out in the wilderness it was not as quiet as in this strange town. At least the howls of coyotes reminded a man that he was still alive.

There was an unholy silence in Anvil City, which did not sit well with the bounty hunter. He stood beside the upright beneath the porch overhang and chewed on the long twisted black cigar as he absorbed everything he could see and hear in the town's main thoroughfare.

Yet there was nothing to either see or hear.

It seemed peaceful enough but the experienced hunter of men had been fooled before. Nothing was ever as it appeared to be. Even though the small town, which he and Squirrel Sally had entered only two hours previously, seemed quiet, Iron Eyes could not shake off the overwhelming feeling that he had missed something.

When you were in his ruthless profession it paid to be cautious. Boot hill was filled with the foolhardy. Iron Eyes had no intention of joining their ranks.

The Devil could wait a little while longer for his rancid soul, he thought.

It had been daylight when he and Squirrel Sally Cooke had arrived in town. Even then they had barely seen more than a half-dozen souls in the town's streets. Iron Eyes recalled that those they had seen had looked frightened. Until now the bounty hunter had assumed that it was the sight of his own horrific face that had put the fear of the Almighty into them; now he was not so sure.

Maybe there was something else.

Iron Eyes had never been to Anvil City before and would have avoided it if it had not been for Squirrel Sally. He had tired of her small hands searching his pants pockets for something he felt she should not be looking for. Sally was young, healthy and spirited, unlike himself. The urge to discover new, unexplored things was a mighty powerful one which

Iron Eyes had never himself experienced. Sally wanted something he had yet to give any female. He had left the pretty girl up in the hotel room alone in a large bed. She would wait vainly for his return.

Iron Eyes had other things on his mind. He wanted to find out exactly what was wrong in Anvil City. Something was amiss. He was certain of that.

But what was it?

The gaunt bounty hunter considered this town to be far too quiet, unless most of its citizens were dead. Iron Eyes turned his attention to the end of the empty street and stared at the hulk of the livery stable. Squirrel Sally's stagecoach stood just outside its wide open doors, whilst the six-horse team was inside, being fed and watered.

His own magnificent palomino stallion was also stabled somewhere inside the large building.

With the cigar gripped firmly in his mouth Iron Eyes stepped down from the boardwalk and started across the wide street towards a lone saloon. Even the saloon did not seem to be anything like any other drinking hole he had seen. It was also as quiet as the night air that chilled his bones. He had never approached a saloon that was so silent before.

Iron Eyes studied the saloon as his long strides drew him closer and closer to it. The lamplight from within its long room spilled out across the sandy street. Yet there was not a single sound coming from beyond its swing doors.

The bounty hunter opened his trail coat to reveal his deadly pair of Navy Colts. They were tucked into his pants belt, ready to be drawn at any moment. Their cold steel pressed against his flat belly. He stepped up on to the board-walk and rested a hand upon the top of the swing doors. A solitary bartender stood behind the long counter. He was the only living soul in the place. Iron Eyes was about to push the swing doors apart when he again sensed that something was wrong.

He paused, turned and stared back at the hotel.

Lamplight of an orange hue spread over the wooden shingles of the porch from one of the hotel's bedroom windows. The thin figure rubbed his chin and thought about the frisky female he had left there on the pretext that he had to go out and buy himself some cigars.

Squirrel Sally was at an age when most females tended to become romantic, or worse. She troubled Iron Eyes more than any deadly outlaw had ever managed to do.

He did not understand her or her yearnings. They were utterly alien to him.

Iron Eyes wondered if he could stay away from her long enough for her to calm down and fall asleep. Few things troubled the long-legged bounty hunter, but she did. He had no understanding of her desire for him. She wanted him the way all ripe females wanted men they had set their sights upon, and it worried him.

Few members of the opposite gender had ever shown any interest in Iron Eyes. He had grown used to their natural revulsion of him. Even before his face had been savagely brutalized they had never really given him a second glance.

Unlike most women, Squirrel Sally did not seem to see his injuries.

She saw something else. She saw and wanted something buried deep within the bounty hunter. What did she see? What could it be about him that made her want him so badly?

Squirrel Sally worried him.

Iron Eyes drew in more smoke and savoured its flavour. Then he was about to enter the saloon when he heard a voice several yards to his right. His left hand instinctively drew one of his Navy Colts from his belt and cocked its hammer as hefty boots closed in on him.

Then he heard panting. It sounded like an old hound dog after a night-long raccoon hunt.

The bounty hunter stepped away

from the swing doors of the saloon and kept his hand firmly on his six-shooter. His index finger curled around its trigger. He was ready to fire and kill if the need arose.

He could see a hefty man rushing towards him through the shadows and lantern-light.

The man called out again. This time more breathlessly. The amber lantern-light danced on a tin star pinned to the man's top coat. Iron Eyes returned his weapon to his belt and stepped towards the approaching lawman.

'Are you calling me?' Iron Eyes asked in a low whisper through cigar smoke.

The well-rounded sheriff was puffing and panting as he staggered up on to the boardwalk.

'Are you Iron Eyes?' he wheezed.

'Yep,' the bounty hunter replied.

'I got me some business for you,' the sheriff said in a desperate tone. 'If'n you're in the mood for some business, that is. I have heard that you got yourself a mighty shapely companion with you in the hotel. She might be more interesting. I sure hope not, though.'

Iron Eyes was curious. There was only one kind of business he knew anything about and that was hunting and killing wanted outlaws. He stepped closer to the rotund sheriff, who had stopped close to the saloon's window and was mopping his brow with the tails of his bandanna.

'You know my business?' Iron Eyes asked.

'Bounty hunting.' Sheriff Higgs nodded. 'Right?'

Iron Eyes pulled the cigar from the corner of his mouth and tapped ash on to the boardwalk. He studied the lawman, who looked far too fat to be a sheriff.

'Right. So this business must have something to do with a critter that's wanted dead or alive, by my reckoning,' the bounty hunter quizzed. 'Right?'

Higgs beamed. 'Exactly. Damn, you ain't as dumb as you look.'

With bony fingers Iron Eyes pushed his long, limp strands of hair from his face. He raised a boot and rested it on the long pole of a hitching rail. 'You got some outlaws you need killing? I only kill men wanted dead or alive. I ain't no stinking hired gunslinger.'

'I know.' Sheriff Higgs rested a hand on the bounty hunter's arm and leaned closer. 'There's three of the varmints, Iron Eyes. All wanted dead or alive. Interested?'

Iron Eyes exhaled a line of smoke. 'Maybe. Answer me this, Sheriff. How come you ain't seen to these three outlaws yourself?'

Higgs looked horrified. 'Me? Do I look the sort that chases wanted outlaws? I can't fight three young hotheads, but you can. Hell, it took me ten minutes to put my boots on. I've heard all about you. I reckon this will be the easiest thousand bucks you ever earned.'

Iron Eyes nodded at the thought of an unexpected payday. 'A thousand bucks. Not a bad reward. Where are these outlaws?'

Higgs turned and pointed to the end

of the street near the livery stable. There were no street lanterns there. The only illumination was a couple of red lamps hanging outside some small houses.

'See the first red lamp?' Higgs asked.

Again the tall man nodded as he sucked smoke from his cigar. 'Yep. I see it.'

'That's where they are.' The sheriff sighed. 'They've bin in there for two whole days. Two days of whoring.'

Iron Eyes walked towards the darkest part of Anvil City with the lawman at his side. 'Who are they?'

Nervously Higgs produced a Wanted poster and handed it to the bounty hunter. Then he watched as Iron Eyes studied it carefully.

'The Brand brothers,' the sheriff said, pointing at the crude images on the poster. 'The most vicious bunch I ever seen.'

Iron Eyes paused close to the two-storey building with the flickering red lamp hanging over its doorway. 'The Brand brothers. I've heard of them. They kill anyone they want to kill when they ain't robbing banks. Did they rob your bank, Sheriff?'

'They would have if we had one.'

Iron Eyes gritted his teeth as he focused on the dimly lit house with its pathetic red lamp. 'Have they done anything besides bedding whores since they arrived?'

'Yep. They killed five innocent people as soon as they got here,' the lawman said. 'Wounded twice as many other folks. I ain't capable of bringing them to book, boy. I'm feared of what they might do when they get bored with the whores in there, though. Ain't nobody safe. Them bastards kill for the sheer fun of it.'

The bounty hunter's theory was vindicated. His suspicions had been entirely correct all along. There was something evil in Anvil City. And it was close.

'I wondered why this town was so quiet.' Iron Eyes inhaled deeply, then tossed his cigar away and began walking. He folded the poster up and pushed it down into his deep coat-pocket, next to his loose bullets. 'Now I know.'

The sheriff worked hard to keep pace with the tall bounty hunter as Iron Eyes strode to a shuttered hardware store opposite the livery stable. He rested his shoulder against one wall and stared at the house that Higgs had indicated.

He screwed up his eyes. Although the blinds of all its windows were pulled down the light of oil-tar lamps managed to escape around their edges.

'They're in there, OK,' Iron Eyes said. 'I can hear 'em.'

'If you say so, Iron Eyes,' Higgs replied, panting.

Iron Eyes checked his guns. 'How many whores do you figure are in there, Sheriff?'

Higgs shrugged. 'A few.'

'How many exactly, Sheriff?' Iron Eyes pressed. 'Don't be coy. You've bin in there before the Brand boys ever arrived in this town. Tell me. How many women are usually inside that house? I gotta know how many women them stinking outlaws might hide behind to protect themselves from my lead.'

'OK. I know of seven gals that work in that house,' the sheriff admitted. 'I think they're all inside there right now.'

Iron Eyes looked concerned. 'That's too many. I don't want to accidently shoot no innocent females by mistake.'

Sheriff Higgs patted the tall bounty hunter's broad back. 'Don't you go fretting none, boy. I'll not press charges against you if a few of them gals get themselves hit by stray bullets.'

'Much obliged, Sheriff.' Iron Eyes glanced down at the tubby lawman and raised an eyebrow before warning, 'I'd take cover if I were you. You're a tad wide and bullets got a habit of homing in on bellies like yours.'

Sheriff Higgs did not require telling twice. For an elderly fat man he ran real fast in the direction of the big livery stable. The bounty hunter smiled, then removed his large spurs and dropped them on to the sand. He cocked one of his guns before moving away from the corner of the store and making his way through the shadows towards the small house.

There was a party in progress inside the whorehouse. A party that was about to take an unexpected turn. As Iron Eyes got within ten feet of the front door he could hear the voices of those inside. The sound resonated through the wooden walls from the bottom to the top of the house. It was impossible to tell where his chosen targets actually were within the building.

Like the skilled hunter he had always been, Iron Eyes moved to the side of the house and squinted into the shadows of the alley that ran its length. He could see three saddle horses in the darkness. He knew that even though the wanted men were having themselves a good time, they were ready to flee at the drop of a hat.

Iron Eyes realized that he had to prevent that at all costs. He had to surprise the Brand brothers and make sure that every one of his bullets found its target.

He stood in front of the door and listened to the joyous activity inside the house.

There were several ways Iron Eyes could put an end to the party and to the three outlaws. He chose the direct one.

Holding one of his cocked guns in his right hand Iron Eyes raised a leg and kicked out violently. The door splintered into matchwood as it was torn from its frame and went crashing to the floor. A cloud of dust rose into the dimly lit ground floor room as Iron Eyes rushed over the shattered remains of the door and swung around when he saw movement out of the corner of his eye. He aimed and then saw that it was only two of the scantily clad females. Faster than seemed humanly possible the bounty hunter turned and fired at a lamp set on a table close to the foot of the stairs. His aim was accurate. His bullet snuffed its flame clean out as it shattered the lamp's glass bowl.

The ground floor of the whorehouse

was shrouded in darkness. That was the way Iron Eyes liked it. He was like a puma and could see perfectly well even in the dead of night.

The females screamed in terror. Maybe it had been the sight of their unexpected visitor before the one lamp had been extinguished that had frightened them. It did not matter to the bounty hunter. He had only one thing on his mind and that was killing the three murderous outlaws who were wanted dead or alive.

Holding his Navy Colt before him he moved silently to the other side of the room. The smell of stale whiskey and cheap perfume filled his flared nostrils. It was a sickening aroma but he ignored it as his honed senses tried to locate his chosen prey.

They must to be upstairs, he reasoned. The trouble was, there were five females with them. Five screaming females whom, he knew, the Brand brothers would use to shield themselves from his bullets.

Iron Eyes moved swiftly to the foot of the staircase, knelt down and listened to the confusion above him. The voices of angry men mingled with the crying and screaming of the women. He could hear movement across the beams that spanned the room he was kneeling in. Then he saw the landing plunged into blackness as the outlaws turned the lamps down. Then he spied two figures on the small landing at the top of the stairs.

The bounty hunter trained the Navy Colt at the shadows. He was about to fire when he heard a pathetic whimpering from one of them. Iron Eyes tilted the barrel of his gun back and waited until he was sure of his target.

He knew that the shadowy figure behind the sobbing woman must be one of the outlaws. Their sort always hid behind the petticoats of women.

'Show yourselves, boys,' Iron Eyes shouted from the blackness that protected him. 'Or are you just too plumb yella?'

None of the infamous Brand brothers answered the bounty hunter's taunt. They would choose to fight in their own way. If it meant using all of the females as shields, that was what they would do. The whores had already done what they were paid to do and were now expendable.

Then Iron Eyes saw a terrified female being pushed towards the very top of the staircase. She was half naked but Iron Eyes did not notice that. All he was concerned about was getting a clean shot at the man behind her. Suddenly a gun appeared from under the woman's armpit. It fired a deafening shot down into the room. Iron Eyes felt the heat of the bullet as it passed within inches of his face.

'That was a mistake, Brand,' Iron Eyes yelled out angrily.

'There's only one *hombre* in this house that's made a mistake tonight, stranger,' one of the outlaws shouted back. 'And that was you.'

Suddenly there were more females on

the landing. They were all screaming as loudly as the two women in the corner behind the kneeling bounty hunter.

Iron Eyes gritted his teeth and was waiting for a clean target to aim at when he heard a noise from just outside the front of the building. It was the sound of one of the men dropping to the ground from one of the upstairs windows.

They were now not only above him: one of them was right behind him in the street. A heartbeat later a volley of bullets came in through the gaping hole in the front wall that the door had once occupied. Lead tore through the back of his trail-coat tails, missing the thin bounty hunter's person only by inches.

No sooner had Iron Eyes realized that he was virtually surrounded than two guns started to blast repeatedly at him from the top of the staircase. Chunks of floorboard were kicked up all around the kneeling hunter. Iron Eyes threw his thin body across the room to where the females were still screaming. He rolled over on to his belly, then saw a gun emerge from under the right armpit of one of the females as she was forced down the stairs. Another bullet came at him and embedded itself in a stout moth-eaten chair next to his shoulder.

Iron Eyes wanted to fire back but knew he still had not seen any of the three men he sought. All he could see was a lot of flesh. Female flesh.

Then the gun fired again. A fiery shaft of fury hurtled across the room. One of the soiled doves behind Iron Eyes was hit and fell against the wall. A line of crimson gore marked the place where she slid down its surface to the floor.

Suddenly Iron Eyes heard the deafening sound of glass shattering to his right. A bullet skimmed just over his head as the outlaw in the street tried to get the bounty hunter in his sights.

Still lying on the floor between two old chairs, Iron Eyes raised his arm and fired his Navy Colt at the hole in the windowpane. He heard the outlaw in the street run away in the direction of their three horses he had seen at the rear of the house.

Iron Eyes looked back at the staircase. He cocked his gun again and searched for a target. Now all of the females were on the stairs. He knew the two other Brand brothers must be hiding amongst the near-naked women.

He crawled towards the far wall, hoping he would get a glimpse of one of the men. All a marksman like Iron Eyes needed was a mere glimpse of a target: he usually managed to hit it.

'Show yourselves,' Iron Eyes yelled out furiously.

All of the females were now at the bottom of the stairs and his targets were somewhere behind them. Even in the darkened room the keen eyes of the bounty hunter could see that the women were being herded across the room towards the gaping hole in the front wall. Then one of the Brand brothers ran out into the street.

Iron Eyes blasted his Navy Colt, but the outlaw had escaped. There was one left, the bounty hunter told himself as he stood and moved towards the five females. They started to scream as the light from outside highlighted the scarred face of the determined man.

Then, as Iron Eyes got within a few feet of the group of screaming women, he caught a glimpse of the man just as the outlaw pushed one of the larger females forward. The well-proportioned woman knocked Iron Eyes off his feet. She landed on top of him. Through the corner of his eyes the half-crushed bounty hunter saw the last of the brothers race out into the street.

It took all of his strength but Iron Eyes managed to heave the woman's hefty form off him. He staggered to his feet. Iron Eyes blasted his Colt again, but it was too late.

Now they were all outside, he told himself.

As he swayed in the centre of the darkened room his long thin fingers reloaded his smoking gun.

'Damn it all!' Iron Eyes angrily cursed himself and swung round to face the street. He snapped the chamber shut and cocked the gun hammer. 'This sure ain't going to plan.'

The frustrated bounty hunter drew his second gun and cocked its hammer as well. Now he had two guns in his hands. He rushed out of the doorway and into the street. He knelt and tried to see where the outlaws had gone. Suddenly he heard a horse galloping through the alley behind him. The rider-less animal collided with the kneeling man. Iron Eyes was knocked heavily into the sand.

The stunned bounty hunter lay on his side and watched as the horse trotted to the nearby livery stable. Then more shots rained in on him from the alley at the side of the building. As the sand was kicked up to both sides of him Iron Eyes crawled to the front of the house and managed to get back up on to his shaky legs. He blasted his weaponry in the direction of the gunsmoke.

For some reason they had stopped shooting.

Iron Eyes searched every shadow for a clue as to where the outlaws were. Then he saw two of them near the livery stable as they passed behind Squirrel Sally's stagecoach. Iron Eyes stepped forward with his guns at hip height and was about to call out to his prey.

Before one word had left his lips he felt something encircling him. It felt as if a snake had ensnared him, but this was no snake. Startled, Iron Eyes looked up as the lasso noose slid up him until it was under his chin and around his throat.

He saw the outlaw in the bedroom window above him. One of them had somehow managed to return to the bedroom with a saddle rope. A fraction of a second later the noose tightened around his thin neck. Iron Eyes felt himself being hauled upward off his feet.

The bounty hunter dropped both his

guns. His hands feverishly reached up and grabbed hold of the rope around his neck in an attempt to stop himself from being hanged.

But he *was* being hanged.

Iron Eyes's boots searched for something to stand upon to take the strain off his neck, but there was nothing close and he was at least three feet above the ground. He could hear the outlaw's laughter as the rope was tied off above him.

He could not swallow. He could not breathe. He was dying and there was nothing he could do. The more he fought the more the rope tightened.

Two more shots were fired at him from the outlaws who had distracted him near the livery. He felt the heat of the hot lead as the bullets tore through his trail coat and grazed his sides. A man with meat on his bones might have been fatally wounded.

Iron Eyes was swinging by his neck above the ground. As his life was slowly being choked out of him the bounty hunter heard the three outlaws' horses thundering away from Anvil City. The Brand brothers had managed to escape the wrath of Iron Eyes. Yet that did not matter any longer to him. Nothing mattered any longer.

A black spinning whirlpool enveloped his mind as he lost consciousness. Iron Eyes's arms fell limply to his sides as he swung by his neck like a monstrous marionette.

From his hiding-place behind a score of empty beer barrels set close behind the Golden Arrow saloon, Sheriff Higgs had listened and watched in horror as the fight inside the whorehouse had spilled out into the street. Then he had witnessed the three outlaws not only lasso a rope around the thin bounty hunter's neck and string him up, but also shoot him.

As the sound of the Brand brothers' horses' hoofs grew fainter the terrified Higgs did something he had never done before in all his years as a lawman. He ignored his own fears and raced out to where Iron Eyes was hanging.

Higgs looked up and stared at the seemingly lifeless bounty hunter swinging in the night breeze with the rope around his neck. The sheriff had never seen anyone hanged before. He did not like the sight.

For some unknown reason he drew his .44 from its holster and cocked its hammer. He raised his arm and aimed as best he could at the rope and fired. His first bullet got the females inside the whorehouse screaming once again, but the lawman ignored their terror.

He fired again and saw his bullet graze the rope. It started to fray as the weight of its victim dragged on its secured length.

The sheriff held the six-shooter in both hands and steadied himself. This time his aim was true. The bullet severed the rope and Iron Eyes fell straight down to the ground.

The bounty hunter's boots hit the sand hard. He fell forward on to his face, right next to the sheriff. Higgs holstered his weapon, knelt, rolled Iron Eyes over on to his back and frantically tried to loosen the noose. The rough rope had cut deeply into Iron Eyes's flesh. At last Higgs achieved his goal and managed to release the rope. There was no sign of life in Iron Eyes's motionless face, but Higgs knew that that did not mean he was dead.

He started to slap the brutalized features. 'Are you dead, boy? Are you? Damn! It's hard to tell with a critter that looks the way you look.'

For more than five minutes the long form of the hideous Iron Eyes did not move a muscle as the frantic lawman continued to slap and punch it.

'Hell! You can't be dead. Not like this,' Higgs grumbled as he began to tire. 'I thought Iron Eyes couldn't be killed like regular folks. Hell! If you weren't so damn ugly I'd bet that you ain't Iron Eyes at all. I don't reckon there'd be another critter as ugly as you are.'

Suddenly the deformed eyelids of the bounty hunter flickered. Higgs scrambled in fear back to his feet as the long bony fingers of the man lying on the ground started to move like spiders.

Then his eyes opened.

The light from the red lamp on the front wall of the house danced on the length of Iron Eyes as he slowly sat up. His eyes darted up to the quivering lawman. There was no emotion in them. It was the look of a dead man before the pennies had been placed over his eyes.

'You OK, boy?' the sheriff asked. 'I had to shoot the rope. It took me a few tries but I got it in the end. Reckon them Brand boys thought they'd finished you off with them shots they fired into you. Lucky you're so skinny. Them shots barely scratched your ribs.'

The bounty hunter dragged the noose from around his neck and tossed it aside. His neck was raw where the rope had tightened and savaged his flesh.

'They hung me,' Iron Eyes croaked.

'Lucky you don't weigh much,' Higgs said nervously.

Iron Eyes carefully turned his head.

'They hung me.'

'They shot at you as well,' the lawman added.

'Nobody does that to Iron Eyes.' The ghostlike creature got to his feet, plucked his guns off the sand and pushed them into his deep pockets. 'They must have reckoned they'd killed me. I heard horses before I blacked out.'

'They high-tailed it.' Higgs nodded. 'Yep. They sure thought they'd finished you OK. If I hadn't have shot that rope I figure you would be dead by now.'

Iron Eyes glanced at the lawman. He could see the smoke trailing from its holstered barrel against the fat man's thigh. 'Much obliged.'

With Higgs at his side Iron Eyes staggered away from the house and the smell of gunsmoke that hung on the night air, towards the livery stable.

'Easy, son. I'll take you over to the doc,' the sheriff said. 'Your neck might be bust. You ought to get it checked.'

Iron Eyes stopped abruptly. 'I don't need no doc. I need vengeance. Them

Brand boys got a lesson coming to them and I'm the one who'll be teaching them it. Savvy?'

'I'll take you back to the hotel then,' Higgs suggested as he studied the unsteady figure beside him. 'You're shaken up, boy. Them Brand boys hanged you, Iron Eyes. You need to rest up a while.'

'Why?'

The sheriff shrugged. 'I don't know. Maybe your head will fall off or something. It's common knowledge that when a man gets himself hung, he needs to rest up.'

Iron Eyes found a cigar and pushed its twisted length into his mouth. He chewed on it. 'How many damn men you met that's gotten themselves hung, Sheriff?'

'None that I've had an argument with afterwards. Except you, Iron Eyes.'

'My throat hurts and my neck hurts even worse,' Iron Eyes said in a low whisper. 'Now I think on it, it was your damn notion for me to try and claim the bounty on them varmints. Some folks would be mighty angry but I ain't. I don't get angry, I get even.'

'With me?' Higgs stared at the tall man who was glaring at him like a rabid wolf. 'I saved your life. You'd still be swinging at the end of that rope if I hadn't shot it.'

Iron Eyes grabbed the lawman's collar and pulled him close. He snorted like a raging bull at the lawman. 'I ain't angry with you. They're the ones who'll have to pay for what they did, Sheriff.'

Higgs gave out a huge sigh of relief.

'Now get my horse. I got me three varmints to catch. I also got me a score to settle.' Iron Eyes snorted.

'What about the little gal over in the hotel?' the sheriff asked. 'Are you just leaving her without telling her why?'

Iron Eyes struck a match and lit his cigar. 'Don't worry about Squirrel. She'll follow me. She always does.'

Sheriff Higgs hurried towards the livery stable as he had been ordered to do.

The bounty hunter rubbed his neck and stared through his cigar smoke at the sand. His eyes narrowed as they found the tracks of the three outlaws' mounts.

'You're all dead men,' Iron Eyes whispered. 'You just don't know it yet.'

1

The sound in the very centre of Rio Concho was deafening as the three out-laws' guns blazed mercilessly. No target was taboo. Men, women and even children dropped to the ground either wounded or dead as the notorious Brand brothers ran down the stone steps from the bank on their way towards their awaiting mounts. Even though there was no return of fire from any of the town's stunned menfolk the gang continued shooting at anyone who caught their eye.

Shafts of fiery red venom exploded from the outlaws' gun barrels and ripped through the dusty air in search of the startled townspeople gathered close to the solid bank building. The sound of echoing gunfire from within the bank had drawn the curious to their fate like moths to a flame. For once the old saying that curiosity killed the cat proved to be lethally correct.

The outlaws threw their hoard of canvas bags filled to overflowing with gold coins across the necks of their horses, then swiftly mounted the animals. No gang of bank robbers ever carried more weaponry than the Brand brothers when they struck. Guns were holstered, rammed in pockets and strung from leather laces that hung from their necks. When one man's gun was empty he instantly switched to another. There was no lull in the shooting. No moment when the deafening racket of deadly gun fire abated.

Still firing their six-shooters, each of the bank robbers tore his reins free of the hitching poles and sat arrogantly astride his horse as they all picked off their defenceless targets with heartless accuracy. From their high perches the demented outlaws found that their killing spree was even easier.

Even more addictive.

This was a turkey shoot. A bloody massacre.

Matt Brand was the eldest of the trio of deadly vermin. His word was law to his two slower-witted siblings Dick and Silas. Matt had always been able to do the one thing they were incapable of doing for themselves.

Think.

He did the thinking for all of them. Matt led and Dick and Silas followed.

Still jubilant over the incident back at Anvil City, the brothers had grown in confidence. Although they had no idea whom they had fought with and triumphed over days earlier, the brothers were now convinced that there was no one who could stand up against them. They wrongly believed that they had executed the bounty hunter and had no idea that Iron Eyes was not to be killed as easily as most men. With every new victim that their guns cut down, Matt Brand became more and more convinced that they were invincible.

Had Brand known that the man they had encountered back in Anvil City was the infamous Iron Eyes and that he had not only survived their bullets and rope but was on their trail, the outlaw might have had second thoughts.

The two younger of the deadly Brand brothers gleefully fanned their gun hammers as the cloud of gunsmoke grew more and more dense. Helpless townspeople fell all around them into the already bloodstained sand.

'Kill as many of them as ya want, boys,' Matt Brand yelled out, swinging his mount around like a victorious general commanding his troops. 'We don't want witnesses this time.'

'Damn. This sure is fun, Matt.' Dick laughed as he forced fresh bullets into his smoking guns. Silas just grunted like a small child who knew he was doing wrong but could not stop himself from enjoying his misbehaviour.

Then Matt looked with deadly intent through their gunsmoke across the street. A street that was littered with dead and dying people. He did not give any of their victims a second thought as his siblings added to the tally. His eyes were fixed on a small wooden structure set fifty yards away from the stone steps of the bank. He spurred and rode across the bodies towards it.

The sign nailed to the wooden structure's porch overhang had one word painted upon its flaking surface.

Matt Brand read the word aloud. 'Sheriff.'

With his brothers close behind him Matt spurred his horse up on to the boardwalk until he was able to knock on the door of the office with one of his smoking Remington .45s.

'What ya doing, Matt?' Silas asked dimly as he and Dick looked on.

The eldest of the Brand brothers chortled. 'I'm gonna kill me a star-packer, Silas boy.'

Both his brothers watched as Matt hammered on the door even harder with his gun barrel. He was determined to get one extra notch on his gun grip. One which he would value more than all of the others carved into the wooden handle of his favourite six-shooter.

Matt Brand kicked out at the door with his hefty right boot as he steadied his mount.

'Are ya in there, Sheriff?' Brand called out before leaning back and fanning his gun hammer at the door until the weapon's hot chambers were empty. The bank robber rammed the smoking gun into its holster and drew another .45 from his belt. He cocked its hammer and levelled the barrel at the bullet-ridden door. 'Come on out, ya damn coward. Come out or I'm riding in.'

No sooner had the words left the bank robber's lips than one of the door panels exploded outward as two rounds of buckshot answered the challenge in kind. A million splinters showered over the three outlaws. The deathly reply had only just narrowly missed Matt Brand's horse. He brought his mount under control and brushed smouldering sawdust from both himself and the gelding beneath him.

'Now I'm angry, Sheriff. Damn

angry,' Brand screamed insanely. 'I'm gonna make sure ya die real slow.'

Bravely the lawman swung what was left of the door wide open. Sheriff Cole Ritter held a twin-barrelled scattergun in his hands. Plumes of smoke billowed from its two large barrels. The lawman quickly raised the hefty weapon just in time to see, hear and feel the bullets that Brand blasted down at him. The impact lifted the sheriff off the ground.

Ritter flew a few feet backwards. Blood squirted up into the air as the lawman crashed into the floor. He lay like a rag doll as his blood surrounded his ample form.

The choking gunsmoke hung like a ghost in the frame of the door. Matt Brand gave out a satisfied howl of delight and yanked at his reins back hard. The outlaw forced his horse backwards until it was standing between those of his brothers in the dusty street.

'Is he dead?' Silas asked, trying to see through the cloud of choking gun-smoke.

'He sure looks dead to me, Silas.' Matt Brand answered, and snorted as he carved a notch in the gun's handle.

'That was damn good shooting, Matt,' Dick said as he steadied his mount next to his elder brother.

Matt Brand looked around the centre of Rio Concho at the bloody mayhem they had created. A satisfied grin filled his unshaven face. Some of the people lying in the sand were twitching. Their arms or legs moved as though unseen heavenly strings were tugging upon them.

Most lay completely still on the sand.

Sand which had turned a sickening shade of crimson.

The trio of horsemen steered their mounts away from the sheriff's office towards the edge of town. Matt Brand could not help himself from looking backward at the savagery they had created in less than five minutes since they had arrived in the peaceful settlement. Then he returned his attention to what lay ahead of them.

'Reckon there ain't gonna be no damn posse trailing our hides this time, boys,' the eldest of the Brand brothers said. 'C'mon. We got a long ride ahead of us.'

The three deadly outlaws spurred.

2

At noon on the following day a wisp of dust on the horizon alerted the still stunned people of Rio Concho that once again a stranger was headed into their stricken town. The bodies of the dead still lay where they had fallen, upon bloodstained sand. A few of the survivors tried desperately to scare away the buzzards, which had been drawn to the stench of death. But the large black birds did not scare easily. Their number had grown steadily the higher the blazing sun got in the cloudless sky. Half of the town's rooftops were covered in them. Each large black bird waited for the slightest opportunity to swoop down and resume its feast upon the dead.

The remaining townsfolk had only just managed to muster enough courage to venture back out into a new day's sunlight. None of the people were the same as they had been less than twenty-four hours earlier. They had been robbed of all their faith and destroyed by what had occurred.

Those who had survived the massacre were in shock.

Their minds could not cope with what had happened. Their brains had stopped functioning. For to think was to remember. Remember things best forgotten. None of them wanted to relive those few sickening moments again. They had never encountered anything like it before. Insanity had paid their remote community a visit. They prayed that it would never return.

Then, one by one, they saw the dust rising from the hoofs of an approaching horse. A wildfire of fear swept through them. They started to scream. Every man, woman and child screamed out in terror. Then they took flight and raced to their homes to hide behind closed and locked doors as the trail dust drew closer.

Only two men dared venture out into the blinding midday sun when they had heard the commotion of hysterical people pass the doctor's home. Doc Richards and the wounded Sheriff Cole Ritter stepped out into the sunlight. The lawman was still groggy from the whiskey his old friend had made him drink before he had cut out two lumps of lead from his massive girth. Yet even Ritter's reddened eyes could see the rider as he rode towards them.

Even with a brain befuddled by hard liquor the lawman knew he had to carry his faithful scattergun, just in case it was the return of the outlaws that they were witnessing.

'Can ya make them out, Leroy?' Ritter asked his friend as he shielded his eyes from the blinding sun. 'Is it them? Is it?'

'You ought to be lying down, Cole,' Richards scolded his patient. 'Them stitches will bust loose if you fire that darn shotgun.'

'Damn it, Leroy. Answer me,' the

sheriff snarled. 'Is it them?'

'Don't think so. I can only make out one rider, Cole,' Richards responded. 'I still reckon you ought to be heading back to the cot in my parlour.'

Ignoring the advice of the man who had saved his life only hours earlier, Ritter pulled back on the hammers of his weapon and then nursed the scattergun across his bloodstained shirt.

'What in tarnation are you doing, Cole?'

'Hush up, Leroy,' the sheriff said. 'I'm thinking.'

Neither man would ever again see his fiftieth birthday, but they had grit. A whole heap of grit. Now all they needed was some luck to go with it. The elderly doctor tilted his head and studied the approaching rider.

'I sure ain't seen him before.' Richards nodded as his old eyes squinted hard at the horseman who had now entered the town and was still heading straight for them.

'A stranger.' The sheriff spat at the

sand. 'I've had my fill of strangers.'

'I sure hope he ain't as bad as them varmints that was here yesterday, Cole,' Richards said with a sigh. 'I'm plumb out of clean bandages and catgut.'

The hoof dust rose up into the sky away from the large handsome horse as it approached them at a steady pace. Then the two figures looked beyond the horse at its master. Neither was expecting the sight which greeted their curiosity.

Both men gasped with horror when they actually saw the rider clearly through the swirling heat haze. Neither man had ever seen anything quite like the horseman before. They both silently thought that most of the dead bodies that littered the street looked in better shape than the man sitting astride the palomino stallion. It was like looking at a corpse on horseback.

'Good grief,' Richards said and gulped.

'Ya right, Leroy,' Ritter stammered. 'He sure ain't one of the *hombres* that shot up the town yesterday. None of them varmints looked that bad.'

Doc Richards looked at his friend. 'I sure hope he ain't wounded, Cole. I'm plumb out of catgut and all.'

The large animal was steered directly towards them. It was in total contrast to its master. The palomino stallion was handsome in its Mexican livery. Its master was anything but gentle on the eye.

Iron Eyes pulled back on his reins and stopped his mount a few feet from the pair of onlookers. He sat and studied the street and its gruesome population of dead bodies. Then his cold bullet-coloured eyes looked down at the two men before him.

He did not speak.

'Who are you?' Doc Richards demanded. 'I've had my fill of folks riding in here killing. If that's ya intention I'd think again. The sheriff here ain't the best of shots but even he can't miss with that scattergun.'

Even with blurred vision Sheriff

Ritter could see the pair of gun grips poking up from behind the rider's belt buckle. He swallowed hard and shook his hefty weapon. 'I might be full of holes but I'll snuff your candle if ya try anything, boy. Hear me?'

The bounty hunter raised both arms and then ran his bony fingers through his strands of jet-black hair until it was off his face. The revealing of the brutally mutilated features stunned both the doctor and the lawman to their very souls.

'Name's Iron Eyes. I'm a bounty hunter,' the horseman said. 'I'm hunting three varmints wanted dead or alive. I trailed them to this town. Looks like they've bin here already.'

Sheriff Ritter lowered his weapon until its twin barrels rested on the ground. He then leaned upon it as though it were a walking stick.

'Three men, ya say?'

Iron Eyes nodded. 'Yep. The Brand brothers. Worth more than a thousand dollars dead. Reckon they must have done this. They hanker after killing as many folks as they can.'

Ritter moved closer to the tall stallion. He overcame his own repulsion and looked up into the horrific face. 'I heard about you.'

'Most folks have.' Iron Eyes nodded and then produced a folded Wanted poster from his deep trail-coat pocket. He shook it open and then showed it to the lawman. 'Recognize any of these likenesses?'

Sheriff Ritter stared at the crude photographic images and focused on the face in the centre of the trio. He jabbed a finger at it and growled.

'That's the critter who shot me,' Ritter raged. 'He must have thought he'd finished me off, but I don't die easy.'

'I don't die easy either, old-timer,' Iron Eyes said. 'He hung me and then his brothers shot at me as I was swinging. Left me for dead.'

Cole Ritter swallowed hard. 'They hung and shot ya?'

'Yep.' Iron Eyes nodded. 'Like I said, I don't die easy.'

'If only you'd arrived here yesterday, Iron Eyes,' Doc Richards said ruefully. 'You look the sort who could have given them Brand boys a run for their money.'

Iron Eyes sighed heavily. 'I would have bin here before they started their killing but my horse threw a shoe. I wasted a lot of time looking for a blacksmith to fix it.'

'They robbed the bank but that wasn't enough for them,' the elderly doctor told him. 'They then started killing and didn't stop until there wasn't anyone left to shoot.'

'They shot me as well,' the sheriff added. 'They cleaned out the bank of all its gold coin. They even killed the bank manager and all of his tellers, Iron Eyes.'

Iron Eyes carefully folded up the Wanted poster and returned it to his bullet-filled pocket. He stared again at the bodies and then down at the two men. 'You're a tad slow cleaning up the dead around here.'

'I seen to the wounded first, Iron Eyes,' Doc Richards told him. 'The dead ain't in any hurry to be tended to. All them poor critters need is a hole.'

The bounty hunter nodded. 'Reckon so.'

'Ya ain't still thinking of trailing them Brand boys are ya, Iron Eyes?' Ritter asked as he continued to study the strange rider. 'They headed west, ya know?'

'So they headed west.' Iron Eyes rubbed his jaw. 'What difference does that make?'

The sheriff pointed at the distant river. 'That's the Pecos, boy. Ain't ya ever heard about it?'

The bounty hunter narrowed his eyes and glared at the river, which he could just make out a few miles from the edge of town. The land that lay beyond it looked no different from a hundred similar landscapes that he had seen before and yet Iron Eyes knew there was a difference. It was said that there was no law beyond the Pecos River.

'I've heard of it.' Iron Eyes produced a cigar from one of his pockets and placed it in the corner of his scarred lips. 'If that's the way they went then that's the way I'm going.'

Doc Richards looked anxious. 'That's the Pecos, Iron Eyes.'

'There ain't no law across that river, boy,' Sheriff Ritter said fearfully. He added a warning: 'For anyone working on our side of the law to head out there is suicide. Ya might as well put a gun to ya head and pull its trigger now. You're a bounty hunter and to the vermin across the Pecos that's as bad as being a sheriff like me. Every varmint in the Pecos is wanted for something and they'll surely kill ya if you follow them Brand brothers into their heartland.'

'Cole's right,' Richards agreed. 'You'll be as dead as these pitiful folks if you ride into the Pecos.'

'They'll kill ya, Iron Eyes.'

Iron Eyes struck a match and raised its flame to his cigar. He filled his lungs with smoke, tossed the match at the sand and toyed thoughtfully with the reins of his tall palomino stallion. He looked at both men as smoke filtered between his small sharp teeth.

'They'll try,' Iron Eyes whispered. 'Folks always try. So far nobody has managed it.'

Both of the elderly men watched as the bounty hunter dismounted in one fluid action. The skeletal figure moved closer to the sheriff.

The nervous lawman backed away a couple of steps.

'What do ya want?' Ritter gulped fearfully.

The emaciated bounty hunter leaned over the shorter lawman and rasped in his ear, 'Where's the saloon, old-timer? I need to buy me some provisions if I'm going into the Pecos. I'm running damn low on whiskey and cigars. Reckon I'll be needing me a whole lot of both if you boys are right.'

'You'll be needing a plentiful supply of bullets as well,' Doc Richards said bluntly. 'If you're loco enough to keep trailing them Brand boys over yonder, that is.'

Iron Eyes blew a line of smoke at the sand. 'I got me plenty of ammunition. Now where's the damn saloon, gents?'

'There. It's over there.' Sheriff Ritter raised an arm and pointed to a saloon set just up an alley opposite them, hidden by a stout tree.

'Much obliged, Sheriff.' Iron Eyes nodded and started to walk with his horse in tow towards the saloon. The sound of his spurs rang out and echoed off the bullet-scarred buildings that surrounded him. With each step he remembered the rope that had nearly broken his neck and the mocking laughter of the men he was still pursuing. Then his attention was drawn to the rooftops as the buzzards began to flap their huge wings nervously. They lifted off the wooden shingles like a black storm cloud and flew away from the sun-bleached town.

Silently the two elderly men returned to the small house belonging to Doc

Richards. They had vainly tried to warn the bounty hunter of the dangers he was about to encounter if he continued his deadly quest. Then they slowly realized that, unlike themselves, some men did not fear death, for it was a constant companion they had grown used to.

Death posed no threat to men like Iron Eyes. Their breed knew it was inevitable in every man's existence that somewhere at some time it would claim them. Life had only one ultimate conclusion. Whatever you did from the time you were born would only change the way death claimed you. It was impossible to prevent that unwanted visitor from eventually taking you. Men like Iron Eyes seemed resigned to that unspoken truth. There was no fear, only acceptance.

It was not a long walk across the street to the saloon but it was a sickening one. The bodies were now covered in flies, which had been drawn to the stench of death just as the buzzards had been. It seemed that even in the middle of an arid desert flies and carrion always managed to appear when something died.

Even to the tall bounty hunter, who outwardly appeared to be entirely emotionless, the scene of so many dead people caused him to pause. He gave none of the dead men a second look but then he saw a woman and a child lying with bullet holes in their backs. Iron Eyes never made war on females and despised those who did.

The tall man sucked on his cigar but there was no comfort in its smoke. He looked around and then saw another female body. She was young. Far too young to have been slain by the Brand brothers' evil lead.

Iron Eyes looped his reins around the tree trunk outside the solitary saloon and tied it firmly. He then walked to where the small child lay and knelt down. She too had been shot in the back. His heart pounded with sadness and rage. He carefully turned her over and stared at the face.

A young, beautiful face. She could not have been more than six or seven years of age. His bony fingers touched her face as though trying to awaken her. The skin was cold though. Icy cold.

A fury engulfed him as he studied her lifeless form for what felt like a lifetime. He dragged his bandanna from his red raw neck and carefully placed it over the child's face. Iron Eyes rose back up to his full height and then slowly returned to his mount.

A million thoughts raced through his mind. Why had he not been able to catch up with the three outlaws before they had reached this small town? Why had his mount thrown a shoe when he had been gaining on the trio of ruthless killers?

Why would they kill females? Why kill children? Why had they killed her?

Suddenly the bounty hunter knew exactly why the Brand brothers were wanted dead or alive. For their kind deserved nothing less than being killed. He resolved that he would find and kill each of them. It would not bring the small girl back to life but it might prevent the outlaws killing another innocent who had yet to lose even her milk teeth.

Iron Eyes dropped his cigar on to the sand and crushed it beneath his mule-eared boot heel.

'They'll pay for that,' Iron Eyes vowed, glancing at the tiny form on the sand. 'Pay with their lives. I promise you that, littl'un. I'll make them pay.'

He inhaled deeply, stepped up on to the boardwalk and pushed the swing doors inward. Iron Eyes headed across the sawdust-covered floor towards the lone bartender. There was a fire in his unholy stare.

A fire that would only be extinguished when he had caught the three outlaws and destroyed them.

'What ya want, stranger?' the bartender asked.

'Whiskey,' Iron Eyes shouted as he banged the bar counter with a clenched fist. 'Six bottles and make it fast. I got me some vermin to kill across the river. And cigars. A box of them if you've got any.'

The bartender found a dusty box of cigars under the counter and laid them down next to the talon-like fingers. He turned to the shelf behind him and plucked one bottle of whiskey after another off its stained surface. He placed each of the bottles on the counter, in front of the thin creature with vengeance brewing inside his heart.

The bartender was about to take refuge at the other end of the long bar when the bounty hunter reached out and caught hold of the man's shoulder. He abruptly turned the man to face him.

'One more thing, friend,' Iron Eyes whispered as he laid a golden eagle down.

The shaking bartender glanced at the horrific face and stammered. 'What?'

Iron Eyes raised a busted eyebrow. 'Is there anywhere in this town where I can buy me some sticks of dynamite and fuses?'

3

The river was low at this time of year. Low and wide. Iron Eyes spurred the magnificent stallion through the fast-flowing water and drew rein when the palomino reached the opposite bank. He glanced back over his shoulder at the peaceful-looking town a few miles behind him. There was no hint that anything had happened apart from the flock of circling buzzards, which were gathering once again. They had returned to feast upon the still unburied bodies. Iron Eyes had followed the trail left by the Brand brothers from the remote settlement to the edge of the river. He studied the soft sand and then spotted their hoof tracks where they had emerged from the river.

The bounty hunter tugged on his reins and forced the large stallion to walk to where the tracks were imprinted upon the otherwise pristine ground. He looked up, then narrowed his eyes and studied the route they had taken. They were headed deep into the Pecos, he reasoned. To a place where they could spend their loot.

A place where he knew he would find even more of their evil breed. Men who deserved to die far more than they deserved to live. A wry grin etched its way across his brutalized face. For all their expertise at killing, the Brand brothers had made one big mistake. One of their victims had not died as they had intended. The most dangerous of their victims had survived and was hell-bent on revenge.

Iron Eyes rammed his spurs into the stallion's flanks and thundered west.

He was headed into an unknown land where he had never been before and, although he had heard all of the spine-chilling tales of what lay within its boundaries, he did not slow his pace.

It was said that this was the burial ground of many good men. Few lawmen had ever managed to escape from this place and those who had were usually left crippled or worse.

Yet in spite of its dark reputation Iron Eyes was unafraid.

It was for those who had yet to encounter him to be afraid.

Unlike so many men who had ridden this way before him, he was no starpacker. Although he rode on the side of the law, he did it for only one reason. He told himself that he did it for the reward money he knew he would earn when he brought in the bodies of those wanted dead or alive. Yet this time it was different, though the bounty hunter did not know it. There was another reason for his determination. One which he could never admit to, for to do so would be to concede he was not the emotionless monster he claimed to be.

It would be proof that he did have feelings buried deep inside his emaciated soul.

He was not hunting a trio of evil men

who had managed to get the better of him. He had no pride to be avenged.

As the gaunt horseman spurred the powerful palomino deeper into the Pecos heartland and his long strands of jet-black hair bounced upon his wide shoulders like the wings of a bat, Iron Eyes could see only one thing in his mind.

It was the pale lifeless face of the small girl he had tried to give a little final dignity by covering her head with his ragged bandanna.

It was a sight that he knew he would never be able to forget, no matter how far he journeyed.

The Brand brothers did not know it yet but their days were numbered, for they were being chased by the man they had hanged and now considered dead. They were being hunted by the creature the Apaches called 'the dead one'. No matter how far the trail of his prey led into the land known as the Pecos he would follow.

He would make them pay the

ultimate price for their outrages. That price was their lives. Nothing else would satisfy the bounty hunter.

He had promised that to a beautiful child and only death itself could stop him from keeping his word.

Iron Eyes rose in his stirrups and thundered on.

4

They had no idea that they were being followed as they entered Splintered Rock. Especially not by a man whom they thought they had already killed. If any of them had known the identity of the man they had lynched back at Anvil City they might have chosen to continue riding. But none of them had even suspected it was Iron Eyes against whom they had battled.

They had survived and that knowledge would not fit with the legend they and all outlaws believed to be true. For Iron Eyes was invincible; it was said that no one ever got the better of him, let alone left him for dead.

None of them had yet realized that they had only fought, but not defeated the notorious bounty hunter; that somehow he was on their trail and closing the distance between them fast.

Men like the Brand brothers had needs. Needs only a certain type of female could willingly provide. For a price, that was. The brothers had the price and Splintered Rock had the women. There was a plentiful supply of that type of female in the outlaw town and they intended buying as many of them as their fortune in gold would allow.

To them the Pecos was a safe haven. Yet even the Pecos was not a place for the three deadly outlaws to rest. Not now. Not with Iron Eyes closing the distance between them with every unceasing stride of his mighty horse.

They were only alive now because the palomino stallion had thrown one of its shoes days earlier and the bounty hunter had been forced to delay his pursuit of them to seek and find someone to reshoe his mount. It was not an easy task to find a blacksmith in the arid prairie, but the resolute Iron Eyes had achieved it. That delay had, however, allowed the brutal massacre in Rio Concho.

The Brand brothers tied their reins to the hitching rail, marched into the Lucky Dice gambling hall and started to spend their recently acquired fortune.

As the three bank robbers started to settled down at a card table whilst near-naked females were paraded before them the doors of the establishment swung open and a filthy bearded man marched in. He approached the brothers.

Curley Jake was one of the few men west of the Pecos who actually worked hard for his money. He was no bandit or bank robber. He was a prospector who had been searching for gold his entire adult life.

The expression on his wrinkled and weathered face was one such as none of the three outlaws had ever seen before. It was the look of triumph. As though he had achieved something he had always been craving for.

Curley Jake leaned on the green baize and stared down at the three men. They in return looked up at their father.

'I done it, boys.' Curley Jake nodded.

'Done what, Pa?' Matt asked as his gaze followed each of the females around their table.

'I found the motherlode. The cave I bin telling ya about all these years.' Curley Jake kept nodding as he vainly tried to contain his excitement. 'I told ya it wasn't no tall story. It's real. I found it after all these years.'

Matt Brand leaned forward and dragged his father's arm until the old man was standing right next to him. 'You couldn't have found it. It don't exist.'

'It don't, huh?' Curley Jake reached into his pants pocket. He withdrew a large nugget of gold and placed it down before his three offspring. 'Then what's that?'

'Is it real?' Silas asked, staring at the rock.

'Fool's gold,' Matt said dismissively.

Curley Jake picked the gold nugget up and sighed as he stared at it in his grubby hand. 'That ain't what they said at the assayer's office, Matt. They said it was the purest nugget they ever tested.'

All three of his sons stood up.

'Where'd ya find it?' Matt asked.

'I found the cave of gold up in the forest, boy. Just like I always said I would. Everyone said I was loco but I found it. It ain't no tall story. It's real. A cave as tall as a church and walls of solid gold.'

'The cave of gold is real?' Dick asked.

'As real as we are.' Curley Jake nodded.

'Where's it at, Pa?' Silas asked.

Before Curley Jake could reply Matt grabbed his arm and, with his brothers following, led the old man back into the street. 'Where in the forest is it?'

'I can take ya there.'

'Then take us there, Pa.'

Curley Jake Brand gave another nod. 'You bet.'

5

The sound of the mighty bullwhip resounded like a series of thunderclaps around the arid prairie as the six horses pulled the weather-beaten stagecoach through a forest of high cactus and twisted Joshua trees. The tiny female chewed on dust as she drove the rocking vehicle across yet another sandy bluff and down into a shaded draw. As the stagecoach rolled down into the first place for over fifty miles to offer a sanctuary from the torturous sun Squirrel Sally brought the long conveyance to an abrupt halt. The dust was choking but Sally did not notice.

She sat upon its high driver's board with her bare right foot on the brake pole as she held the long heavy leathers in her small hands. With the sun no longer burning the flesh from her bones Sally was able to relax for the first time since she had left Anvil City days earlier. She dropped the bullwhip down into the driver's box and gave out a long exhausted whistle.

She studied the terrain that faced her with a mixture of curiosity and concern filling her tiny frame. She looped the long reins around the pole, then lifted her small filthy foot from its splintered length.

Sally was tired but would never admit it, not even to herself. She leaned back against the luggage rail and inhaled deeply as her bones began to settle back to where they were meant to be. Hours of holding on to the reins of six powerful horses as they tried to tear free had a habit of ripping the sinews of even the strongest of souls.

She hurt. Hurt really bad.

There was no way she could have managed to get this far if she had not been fuelled by a large dose of anger. Most females, no matter how young or old they happen to be, can move mountains when their dander has been ruffled by a man. Squirrel Sally's dander was well and truly ruffled.

She lay back, closed her eyes and tried to calm herself. That was quite impossible for someone as young as she. She had been wronged. Not because the man of her choice had taken advantage of her but because he still had *not* taken advantage of her. No matter how hard she had tried to light Iron Eyes' fuse, she had failed.

Rejection was a bitter pill, no matter how much sugar it was coated with.

Squirrel Sally had no intention of accepting defeat gracefully. She would never allow anything she had caught to escape. She had caught the bounty hunter even if he still did not know it.

The female knew she would have to feed and water her team soon if they were going to be able to keep up with their mistress's demands. She intended to keep trailing the tracks left by the powerful palomino stallion until she reached a town. Maybe then she would get her hands on the skittish Iron Eyes again.

Her skin glistened as droplets of sweat trailed from her face and fell on to her torn shirt. She blew a strand of her hair off her face and stared down at her barely concealed chest. The shirt clung to her like a second skin. There was nothing beneath her clothing that could not be seen through the wringing wet fabric.

She forced herself back up until she was resting her elbows on her knees. No winter downpour could have drenched her as completely as her own perspiration had done, yet she gave it no mind. There were other, more important things festering inside her beautiful head. All hunters felt trepidation when they were in unfamiliar territory.

Where the hell am I? Sally wondered. She picked up her Winchester and cranked its mechanism, sending a brass casing flying from its magazine over her shoulder before forcing gleaming new bullets into its magazine. She did not like this place, wherever it was. She had no knowledge of what wild animals roamed through the desolated prairie.

Her imagination was on fire. Could there be creatures here that she had never even heard of? Things that were bigger than bears and more lethal than cougars? Could there? Her tiny hands rested the repeating rifle beside her on the seat. She then thought about Iron Eyes again. 'Where's he headed? Damn it! He ain't nothing but grief. Two-legged grief. I sure wish he didn't love me so much.'

Days of sleepless trailing were taking their toll. The fury inside her was like a volcano about to erupt, but the young woman was determined to remain in control. She pulled out her corncob pipe from her pants pocket and blew down its stem before hammering it on the plank of wood she was sitting on. Then she started filling its bowl with tobacco from her leather pouch, which was hanging on the brake pole. With each action her eyes darted nervously around her and absorbed every detail of the unfamiliar landscape she had trailed Iron Eyes to. But her senses were dulled because even the youngest and fittest of souls need to sleep at some point during each day. Squirrel Sally had stubbornly refused herself that simple gift. The gift of rest.

It had made her uneasy. Her nerves were on edge. The heat haze before her had started to become more than simple hot shimmering air. Now it was as though everywhere she looked she thought that she had seen something which did not actually exist.

This satanic place was unlike anything she had ever experienced. To her weary mind it was as though during the hours of darkness, as she had kept cracking her bullwhip and forcing her exhausted team of horses to continue charging ahead in pursuit of the bounty hunter, she had somehow managed to travel into Hell itself.

This must be Hell. Sally was becoming more and more convinced of that impression with every passing moment. Maybe she was dead? Maybe this was nothing more than some strange trick

79

the Devil taunted all of his victims with.

The youngster was troubled and rubbed her sore eyes. How would anyone know they were dead? She shuddered and her teeth gripped the pipe stem firmly.

Sally dragged a match across her filthy pants leg, cupped its flame above the tobacco-filled pipe bowl and sucked. She sucked hard and frantically. Smoke billowed from the bowl of the pipe, as well as her mouth, before she rested it down against her muscular thigh.

She had driven her team through the night and halfway through another day but still there was no sign of the man she hunted. Where was her beloved?

Her man.

Iron Eyes.

Only his horse's hoof tracks told her that she was still on his trail. No matter how hard Iron Eyes tried he could never escape her. She, like the infamous bounty hunter, was a skilled hunter herself. Few could ever equal the tracking skills of either of them.

The hoof tracks of the palomino were

branded into her memory. Even darkness could not conceal them from her
knowing eyes. She would follow them
until there was no life left in her body,
she resolved.

Even though the six sturdy horses
were exhausted and ready to drop, their
mistress had other plans. She was as
stubborn as the man she hunted and
would never willingly quit, even if it
cost her every one of the spent animals.

Her petite hands reached down into
the deep box beneath the driver's board
and felt for her saddle-bags. She hoisted
them up and pulled out a bottle of
whiskey from a nest of many other
identical bottles.

She might have been young but she
knew that the one weakness her man
had was hard liquor. Even though he
had never been able to get drunk like
normal men, Iron Eyes had a thirst for
whiskey which he was never able to
quench no matter how much he poured
down his throat.

It was the bait Sally had used many

times before to reel him in. It was like an angler's hook. She rested the bottle on her knee and once again studied the land before her. A land which seemed to stretch on for ever and lead nowhere.

Was this Hell? Had she somehow left the real world and been drawn into Satan's lair? Her mind needed rest but she refused to acknowledge that stark possibility.

Sally yawned. She did not know it but she desperately needed sleep. An awful lot of sleep. Her mind had already started playing tricks with her.

Reality and illusion blurred in her young weary brain.

Squirrel Sally rubbed her eyes, blinked hard and vainly attempted to make sense of the situation she found herself in. Why was Iron Eyes heading into a land that seemed devoid of anything but sand and strange plants?

It confused her already tired mind. And why had he left her waiting for him to finally consummate their unwritten betrothal?

'Why are ya riding this way, Iron Eyes?' Sally shouted as she kept looking beyond the heads of her lead horses at the tracks left by the big palomino stallion. 'Ain't nothing here but sand and weird-looking trees with more spikes on 'em than ya find on a porcupine's butt.'

She withdrew the cork from the whiskey bottle's neck and took a long swallow of the fiery amber liquor. She shuddered and returned the cork. Her eyes squinted, and then she saw the other hoof tracks spread out around the fresher ones left by the palomino.

'So ya hunting someone, huh?' She nodded to herself. 'They better be worth a whole lot of money or I'm gonna skin ya alive.'

She puffed furiously on the pipe and then coughed like an old man. Her thoughts returned to the last time she had seen Iron Eyes.

She fumed and then shook her fists at the air.

'And how come ya left me back at Anvil City, ya worthless streak of bacon?'

Sally yelled out as if Iron Eyes could actually hear her tirade. 'Leaving ya betrothed like that is a hanging matter in some parts. There I was, waiting in my bed in that darn pricey hotel room, and you heads on down to get some cigars. I'm still waiting for ya to come back, Iron Eyes. Where in tarnation is ya going to buy them cigars?'

Sally was about to increase her emotional ranting when her finely honed instincts warned her she was not alone. The fine hairs on the nape of her neck tingled. There was someone or something close, she thought. Very close. For a moment the youngster wondered if her tired mind was playing even more tricks with her.

Then she heard the sound of dried brush being broken by something treading upon it. She looked all around her. Then she saw a shadow cross before the front of her team from high above. It had come from the ridge to her right.

Something was moving, she told herself.

Something which if its shadow was anything to judge it by, was big. High above her over the dusty ridge the sound of dry brush snapping underfoot again filled the air.

'I ain't alone.' She grabbed her rifle and swung its barrel around until it was aimed at the ridge and the unseen visitor just over its rim. Every instinct in the small female was now aflame and ready for action.

This was no dream. This was really happening, she thought.

Either an animal or a person was up there. Either way she sensed trouble. Big trouble. This was no place in which to get tangled up in a fight. Sally stared along the length of the rifle's barrel as her index finger teased the weapon's trigger. She could shoot the eye out of a squirrel at a hundred yards when she was rested, but now she was tired. Her eyelids kept closing and she had to raise her eyebrows high in order to fend off the sleepiness which still hampered her.

Doubts began to creep into her mind

again. Was this real? Or just a dream? Was she really here in the middle of a prairie, or was she still in that soft hotel bed back at Anvil City? How could she tell?

She grabbed the bottle, took a quick swig of its fiery contents and blinked hard. The whiskey sure tasted real.

'Something did make a noise up there and it wasn't no damn squirrel,' she whispered to herself whilst she waited for another sound to betray the unseen creature's position. Then the snap of more dried branches filled the air.

If this was a dream or a nightmare it was a very complicated one, Sally reasoned. She had never had any dreams which got this annoying before.

The hunter in Squirrel Sally had already realized that there might be strange wild animals in the prairie, but even her tired mind doubted any of them would be clumsy.

She inhaled and then shouted at the top of her lungs.

'Come on out, whoever ya are. I'm

just itching to blow somebody's head clean off.'

There was an eerie silence which seemed to last an eternity to the young female with the cocked Winchester in her hands. Yet she was a hunter and would wait for as long as it took to bag her prey. Time meant nothing to those who lived their lives by killing.

She could wait for as long as it took, but she knew that sometimes you could frighten your prey into seeking protective cover. If this was a wild animal it might be worth killing and cooking. She was hungry.

'Ya heard me,' Sally yelled out again as she balanced on her knees upon the stagecoach driver's board. 'Show yourself or I'll surely come looking for ya. I kill the critters I hunt. Kill, skin and eat 'em.'

This was no idle threat. It was true.

Then she heard the sound of a horse snorting just over the ridge. A horse in this kind of territory usually meant a rider was sitting upon it, she correctly reasoned. There were no wild mustangs within a hundred miles of here. If there were she had not set eyes on them.

With the rifle still trained at the place from where she had heard the noises coming from Sally jumped up on to the top of the coach and walked along its roof. She listened hard and could hear the horse more clearly now from her higher elevation.

She paced back and forth on the roof of the stagecoach like a mountain cat trying to get a glimpse of its chosen prey.

To her utter frustration whatever was making the taunting sounds that had alerted her that she was not alone in this remote place managed to remain just out of sight over the rim of the sandy rise.

'Horses don't travel this unholy land on their lonesome,' Sally said to herself as her finger remained on her rifle trigger. 'I know ya up there, ya yella bastard. Best show yourself or I'll start shooting.'

Sally was about to shout again when

she recognized a familiar noise on the ground behind her. It was the sound of a six-shooter. She stopped pacing. Squirrel Sally remained quite still. The rider had circled her, she angrily thought.

The gunman had left his horse on the ridge to distract her and had then managed to get behind her.

An ice-cold chill traced up her spine.

'Damn it all!' She sighed angrily and stomped her small left foot on the stagecoach rooftop. 'This ain't good.'

'Don't make no sudden moves, missy,' the man's voice warned from behind her. 'Drop that toothpick nice and easy. Don't make no sudden moves or I'll have to shoot.'

Squirrel Sally remained motionless for a few seconds on the roof of the stagecoach. She listened to the boots of the man moving across the sand. Her mind raced. What should she do? She had heard his gun being cocked. It had to be aimed at her back. There was only one reason to cock a six-shooter and that was to use it.

She was the target. The prize was probably her stagecoach and its six-horse team, she told herself. They would probably bring a good price somewhere in this unholy land.

She slowly lowered the Winchester from her shoulder until it was at hip level and listened to the footsteps coming closer and closer behind her.

What would Iron Eyes do? she silently asked herself.

There seemed to be only two options. Kill or be killed.

The boots stopped their progress. Whoever it was had a cocked gun in his hands and more than likely it was aimed at her back, she told herself. Could she turn and fire faster than it took for the gunman to squeeze his trigger? There was only one way to find out.

She swallowed hard, summoned every last scrap of her resolve and swung round as fast as she could manage without falling from her high perch. Her narrowed eyes saw the figure clad entirely in black with the cocked gun in a gloved hand held at arm's length. Whoever he was his face was hidden by the shadow of a wide flat-brimmed Stetson; it was impossible to make out any features.

A thousand thoughts raced through her young mind in the time it took for her heart to take just one beat.

Squirrel Sally was about to fire when she saw and heard his six-shooter explode into action. A cloud of gunsmoke tore through the air. A bullet sped up towards her. Sally ducked but it was too late.

She felt the impact of the bullet as it collided with the metal barrel of her trusty rifle. Sparks splintered in all directions.

It was like being kicked by a mule.

The sheer force sent her Winchester soaring heavenward as she herself was knocked off her feet. Sally flew backward off the roof of the stagecoach.

The young female was swimming but there was no water, only air. Her arms and legs flapped frantically as she attempted to grab hold of something to stop her fall. But there was nothing to grab hold of except gunsmoke.

She somersaulted and saw the ground draw closer to her as she fell. Squirrel Sally closed her eyes and crashed into its unforgiving surface. Every scrap of wind was forced from her youthful frame by the violent impact.

She lay face down, stunned and helpless.

Sally tried but could not move a muscle. It felt as though every bone in her tiny body was shattered into a thousand fragments.

Bravely Sally lifted her head slightly and then heard the chilling sound of the boots as they steered a course directly towards her supine body. Fine granules of sand were crushed beneath the hefty footwear as a dark shadow stretched across her outstretched arms.

For the very first time in her short life Squirrel Sally felt utterly helpless and unable to protect herself. Her sand-filled eyes stared at the shadow a few inches from her. She could see the smoking gun in the shadowy hand.

Her heart raced.

Where was her beloved Iron Eyes? She needed him now more than she had ever done. Whoever had shot her rifle from her hands would not stand a chance against Iron Eyes, she silently told herself.

Again she tried vainly to move.

The gunman had walked around the back of her stagecoach until he was only a few feet from her. She blinked hard and managed to turn her head towards the eerie figure. Sally wanted to see the face of the bushwhacker but it was impossible.

The sun was directly behind his towering form.

Squirrel Sally could see nothing through her dazed eyes but the black shape of the creature and the smoking gun in his gloved hand.

A gun which was aimed right at her head.

Then to her horror she heard the sound of his gun being cocked again.

6

There was a deep furrow in the sand where the small female had landed heavily after falling from the top of her stagecoach roof. Slowly the numbness which had come over her after her violent encounter with the ground began to ease. A strange sensation flowed through her from head to toe. With it came pain. A thousand fire ants could not have done a better job at tormenting her bruised body. She could taste blood in her mouth and then her hands began to sting. Sally blinked hard and looked at her digits. They were the colour of raw steak where her rifle had been torn from her hands by the stranger's bullet. She tried to count her fingers but could not focus clearly.

Although stunned the feisty female knew exactly what was happening. She had heard the sound of the gun being cocked only seconds after the shadow of her adversary had crossed over her. Sally knew he was standing over her with his six-shooter probably aimed at her helpless body.

Squirrel Sally had waited for the gun to be fired for what felt like hours but in truth was only a few moments. Her weary mind wondered if she would hear the bullet that ended her existence, or was it true that no one ever hears the bullet that kills them?

Was it true?

She felt that soon that question would be answered.

The man was motionless, like a statue. She stared at the shadow as blood trickled from the corners of her mouth. He had not moved a muscle since coming to a halt beside her. For some reason the figure that loomed over her did not squeeze his trigger.

Why?

Why did he not end her misery? Was he torturing her? Was this some sort of sick game he was playing with her? Was he the cat and she the mouse?

He was going to make her wait until he chose the time to fire his weapon. Maybe that was how he liked it. It was power, she thought. The hunter always had the power over the hunted. It was what some folks enjoyed. They did not kill for any true reason, but simply because they could. It was power. Power over those who were unable to defend themselves. Unable or not allowed to defend themselves.

Sally's mind raced as it began to pound like an Apache war drum. He still had not squeezed the trigger.

Was this man one of those who enjoyed hurting others? A creature who got his sick pleasure from torturing his victims before he blew their heads apart?

Was that to be the final indignity she would have to suffer? Maybe he wanted her to beg for her life? If so, he would die of old age before hearing her beg, she thought. Then a more troubling idea filled her pounding mind. Perhaps he had other plans for her. More carnal plans. She was a lone female, after all. A lone female in a land where women were mighty scarce.

Fear raced through her.

Maybe the mysterious gunman had noticed her from his secret hiding-place. Noticed the sweat-soaked shirt that clung to her small perfectly formed breasts. Maybe he had an itch which only bedding a female could cure. She was now even more afraid than she had been when she had heard the gun being cocked above her.

Again she blinked and tried to clear her mind of the swirling thoughts that taunted her. She was so tired. She wanted to close her eyes and sleep for a thousand years. Maybe this was nothing more than a cruel nightmare, she pondered.

Sally wanted to scream but knew that she was only still alive because he had not squeezed on his trigger yet. If she called out he might decide to silence her permanently. Then he could do exactly what he wanted to do with her.

Alive or dead, she was still a female. Some men would bed anything that remotely resembled a female. The dull pain inside her head persisted.

Squirrel Sally closed her eyes and rested her temple against the sand. Why had he not ended her torment? This was worse than being dead. The wait seemed to be lasting for ever.

Then she heard him take one more step towards her. Was this it? Was this the end? Then, to her surprise she heard the sound of the gun hammer being released back down. Then came the distinctive noise of metal against leather as the weapon was holstered.

Without warning a gloved hand grabbed her long, unkempt hair. Savagely her face was dragged up from its resting place. She thought her neck would break as he shook her like a rag doll. Defiantly Sally spat the sand from her mouth. She twisted and wriggled and tried to see his face.

Yet it remained bathed in shadow.

'Let go of me, ya stinking galoot.'

'I thought you were dead, missy,' the chilling voice said from behind her as the hand continued to haul her up by her mane of long hair until she was on her knees. The hand released its grip. Sally rocked on her knees and managed to raise her left hand to rub the sand from her face.

'Who are ya?' she growled.

There was no answer to the simple question. The figure walked around her as though studying her carefully. She tried to keep her eyes fixed upon him but she was too giddy. She wiped the blood from the corners of her mouth and then realized she had bitten her tongue when she had landed face first on the ground. Sally exhaled loudly and lowered her head until she was looking down at herself. Only when her eyes cleared did she notice that what was left of her shirt front had lost half its buttons, revealing her chest. Sally pulled both sides of the shirt together to cover her modesty.

'Why'd ya ambush me?' Sally asked angrily. 'Things must be real slow for anyone to ambush an innocent young female like me.'

The figure stopped abruptly, looked in her direction and gave out a grunting laugh. 'I didn't ambush you. You stopped the stagecoach and I came to investigate to see if you were who I was told you were. As far as being an innocent female that ain't what I've heard about Squirrel Sally. Anyone who rides with Iron Eyes can't be that innocent.'

'What?' She moved her head and heard her neck click loudly. For a moment she did not move for fear of her head falling off her slim neck. When convinced it was not going to do so she realized that most of her bones seemed to have returned to where they were meant to be. Sally turned her beautiful eyes upon the man who kept his wide-brimmed hat pulled low over his face. 'Ya know my name? How'd ya know my name?'

'I've bin following you, missy,' he admitted. 'Ever since you left the hotel back at Anvil City.'

'Why?' Squirrel was curious. 'Nobody follows me. Not unless they got plans to ambush me and steal my stagecoach and team. You can't fool me. That's what ya really want. My horses and my stage. Admit it.'

The figure's long legs paced a wider circle around her. She then saw the one thing that she had not noticed about him before. Whoever this man was, he had only one arm. His empty right sleeve was turned up and pinned to the fabric close to his shoulder.

'I ain't after your stage or them nags,' he drawled.

'Then why'd ya follow me?' She managed to force herself off the sand and stood for a few moments before resting her aching body against the wheel of the large stagecoach. 'Why'd ya hold me up and shoot me?'

'You ain't shot,' he said drily. 'You were gonna shoot me though, missy. I had to shoot that carbine out of your hands before you did. It ain't my fault you fell off the roof of the damn stage.'

Squirrel Sally was still confused. She tried to think but all she could do was stare at the man's empty sleeve.

He moved closer to her.

'You noticed my missing arm,' he observed. 'That's part of the reason I've bin trailing you since you left Anvil City.'

'I ain't got ya damn arm.' She raised her head and stared at him as he moved closer to her. At last she could see his face. It was a face that did not match the voice. He was far older than he sounded, with grey sideburns that reached his jawline.

'Where's Iron Eyes?' he asked.

'Is that why ya bin following me?' Sally again queried. 'Are ya after my betrothed?'

'In a manner of speaking I am.'

'Why are ya after Iron Eyes?'

His eyes lowered until they were staring at her young, beautiful body.

'That's between him and me, missy.'

Squirrel Sally stared at him hard. 'So ya bin trailing me knowing that I'd more than likely lead ya to him. Right?'

'Yep.'

'If ya thinking about hurting him ya best think again, mister,' she warned. 'I'll kill ya myself if ya harms a hair on his head. He's my man. We're gonna get hitched.'

'Me and Iron Eyes got us unfinished business.' He shrugged and stood directly before her. Far closer than she liked. She could feel his breath on her exposed damp flesh. His eyes were studying her the way a hungry man studies an inch-thick juicy steak. He was devouring her with his eyes. 'I was told that you're his woman.'

She covered her bare breasts with her hands and tried to pull the ripped material together. It made little difference though. What was left of the damp shirt was virtually transparent. Sally cleared her throat to get his full attention.

'I'd appreciate it if ya looked me in

the face when ya gabbing, mister,' Sally snorted. 'This body is for the eyes of only one man. My man. So keep ya eyes off my chest.'

The man smiled. 'He's a lucky man.'

She nodded in agreement. 'He sure is.'

The man raised an eyebrow. 'Tell me. Where is Iron Eyes, missy?'

Suddenly she felt concerned. 'What ya want with him? You admitted that ya was trailing me to get to Iron Eyes. What ya want with my betrothed?'

The man smiled but did not reply. He turned and slowly walked away from her towards the sandy ridge. As he reached her rifle he bent down and picked it up off the sand. He threw it across the distance between them and nodded as she caught it.

'What's ya name?' Sally asked. 'I'll tell Iron Eyes that ya looking for him when I catch up with him.'

'The name's Wolfe. Wolfe with an e.' The one-armed man touched his hat brim, then climbed up the ridge and disappeared from view over the sandy rise.

'Wolfe with an e.' Sally repeated the name. 'What kinda dumb-ass name is that?'

Squirrel Sally held the repeating rifle in her grazed hands and then heard the sound of a horse galloping away. She rushed to the front of the six-horse team and watched as the rider galloped into the prairie. Wolfe was heading in the same direction as Iron Eyes' track led.

'I ain't sure that I trust that one-armed critter,' Sally muttered to herself. 'I never heard Iron Eyes mention anything about him having a friend with only one arm. If he ain't a friend then he might just be an enemy. Iron Eyes sure got himself a lot of them. I'd best feed and water the team if I wanna have me a chance of catching up with that Wolfe critter.'

She turned and walked back to the coach. Her grazed hands opened its door. The still weary female reached in for the sacks of oats she had stacked inside. She hauled one of the sacks towards her and then felt a cold shiver trace the length of her backbone. 'What if that one-armed varmint catches up with Iron Eyes before I can warn the skinny critter someone named Wolfe is looking for him?'

As the bruised and aching Squirrel Sally made her way along the team of horses and started shaking oats on to the ground in front of each of them her attention was drawn to the sun-drenched prairie stretching ahead. She stared in horror at the dust from the rider's horse as it rose up into the cloudless blue sky.

Wolfe was now thundering across the prairie. She could see the rider whipping the horse's tail with the long lengths of his reins. He was a good horseman for someone with only one arm, she thought.

Too good.

Sally swallowed hard as her heart began to race. 'Damn it all. He's found my beloved Iron Eyes' trail. He's gonna catch my man before I can get this damn stage moving again. There ain't no time to lose.'

Whoever the mysterious one-armed Wolfe was, he was now a long way ahead of her. Squirrel Sally knew she had to feed and water her team quickly. There was no time to waste.

A man named Wolfe was hunting the hunter.

7

There were two kinds of gunfire. One was the kind drunken cowboys favoured when they were joyously spending their monthly wages, and the second was the kind that sent men to their Maker. There were few who could tell the difference from a distance but Iron Eyes was one of them. He had heard a few random shots as he closed in on the remote town set in the very depths of the Pecos, but he knew that none of them had been fired in anger.

Iron Eyes stopped the palomino for a few endless seconds and stared at the town's crude sign. The board was of simple construction. Two nails held it all together and countless bullet holes ventilated its surface.

'Splintered Rock,' Iron Eyes read aloud. He struck a match with a thumbnail and touched the end of the cigar gripped between his teeth. He inhaled and stared ahead. He could smell the town even though he could not yet see it. The acrid stench of a hundred outhouses in need of lime dust told him that he had found the place he knew the Brand brothers had headed for after committing the outrage back across the river at Rio Concho. 'Smells like a friendly little cesspit.'

Iron Eyes glanced down and inhaled deeply as his eyes focused upon the three sets of hoof tracks in the sand. They led towards the putrid aroma.

The bounty hunter spurred on.

There were few towns across the wide Pecos River where the law had managed to take root. At the best of times there were less than a dozen lawmen spread out within 500 square miles of the fast-flowing waterway. A few federal marshals vainly tried to fill the gaps between one lawless outpost and another, but at least half of their number were as bad as those they were meant to be hunting.

Splintered Rock was a settlement built by lawless men who wanted a place where they could do exactly as they wished. A place where they could gamble and drink as much as they wanted as well as enjoy the charms of as many generously endowed females as their budgets would allow. It was also a place where the only law was gun law. The fastest and most accurate gunslingers were the territory's kings.

Folks tended not to waste a lot of time arguing with one another in Splintered Rock. They drew their guns and shot first and no one batted an eyelid.

Each killer was confident that there was no sheriff or judge to put him on trial. There was no risk of having your neck stretched for simply killing someone in this remote settlement.

To kill or be killed for little or no reason was something that each and every one of those who lived west of the Pecos had grown used to. It was a price only a certain breed of person was willing to pay.

Few good men ever rode across the Pecos and survived.

This was a place where bad men ruled.

They had no desire for civilization to start smoothing off its rough edges. Splintered Rock was where men knew that they might not live as long as those who did not rely on their shooting skills to protect them and yet they did not give a damn.

To live for five minutes as a real man was thought to be worth the risk. Most men spent decades slowly dying as they were browbeaten into submission by the faceless creatures who liked nothing more than controlling others. It did not work west of the Pecos. The lawmakers who never seemed to be satisfied did not find favour here. They had tried and failed to turn Splintered Rock into another town like so many others, filled with law-abiding people. But the people who had created this town did not like either the law or those who made the laws. Bullets had always managed to do their talking for them and that was how these people liked it.

The gun-toting creatures who roamed Splintered Rock defied every known law and were willing to die for the privilege of being free. Yet sometimes the lawless made the innocent pay a price that was too high.

Just as the small child back at Rio Concho had done. She had been senselessly murdered, and it had had nothing to do with freedom. There was an invisible line and the Brand brothers had crossed it. There was only one man who was willing to risk everything in order to right that wrong.

Iron Eyes.

Splintered Rock lay between two gigantic boulders which had at some time in the past actually been one. The rock had cracked up its centre and fallen apart, leaving an almost flat area in between. This was where the town had been built. A vast prairie surrounded the town, giving no hint of the settlement's existence. Beyond the prairie a huge untamed forest covered the lower slopes of a mountain range which appeared to stretch from one horizon to the other.

The forest was where, unknown to the approaching bounty hunter, Curley Jake Brand had led his three sons to show them the vast cavern filled with gold that he had discovered.

The town never rested for even a heartbeat. Day and night were exactly the same to those who burned their fuses at both ends. Unlike their more respectable Eastern cousins they did not live their lives looking at clocks.

Time meant nothing to those who knew they did not have as much of it as honest law-abiding people. Each beat of their soiled hearts might be their last and they all wanted to enjoy those precious moments before a bullet or a knife took it away from them.

Yet, even knowing each moment might be their last, none of the town's inhabitants was prepared to change one thing about their putrid lives. To them they had created paradise on earth. It would not take long for the people of Splintered Rock to learn that even here they were not safe from the infamous Iron Eyes.

He was unlike any other man they had ever encountered. Even their worst nightmares had never conjured up anything to equal the dogged bounty hunter as he entered the untamed town. He was like a bloodhound on the trail of a raccoon. The Brand brothers were his prey and he was never going to quit his hunt until he had found them.

The late afternoon breeze sent dust rolling down the twisted streets of Splintered Rock, as was its daily ritual. The town's riders chewed on it as they navigated from one saloon or whorehouse to another. The streets were busy as fallen angels and fresh clients alike mingled in readiness for nightfall.

The town was bustling even though it never truly came to life until after sundown. Hundreds of people milled around the settlement. Every one of the men wore a gunbelt with at least one well-oiled six-shooter holstered and ready for action. Most of the females also carried weapons, although they tended to conceal them either in bags or tucked into their garters beneath layers of soiled petticoats. Men and women alike were loaded for bear.

Even so, none of them noticed or paid any attention to the hideous stranger who rode through the dust atop his high-shouldered palomino stallion. Without seeming to move even a muscle the thin horseman steered his mount between the people and horse-flesh along the wide busy thoroughfare.

The emaciated rider looked more dead than alive, but that was nothing unusual in Splintered Rock. Most men looked the worse for wear when they ventured out into the sunlight. He kept his chin low and allowed his long black hair to conceal his face. His eyes peered through the long limp strands that hid his facial injuries from view.

Every fight Iron Eyes had survived was carved into his flesh. His face bore the scars of a lifetime of battles. It no longer resembled the faces of other men. It had been mutilated until it resembled badly stitched saddle leather rather than the skin of a man.

Iron Eyes kept on guiding the tall stallion with slight movements of the reins between his left thumb and index finger. The animal responded. The rider watched everyone, men and women alike. He showed no favouritism. Iron Eyes knew that even the most innocent-looking of females could kill as easily as the most obvious gunfighter.

His eyes darted from behind the veil of long black hair as it moved with the breeze. He was only too aware that if any of the town's people recognized him as a deadly bounty hunter they would start shooting.

But none of them took any notice of the stranger who was now riding through the very middle of their town.

Iron Eyes had lost sight of the hoof tracks of his prey as soon as he had reached the first of the town's houses.

The streets were churned up from constant traffic, both human and horse. His eyes darted for any sign of recognition that the stranger who was now in the town's main street was not like any other horseman who had ever dared enter Splintered Rock before.

But there was none.

Every one of the people who filled the crowded street knew that bounty hunters and lawmen never came here. Perhaps that was why nobody seemed interested in him. They could never imagine that someone on the side of the law would be either brave or crazy enough to enter their town.

They were blissfully unaware that he was not an outlaw seeking refuge to spend his ill-gotten gains, as so many of them were. They had no idea that he was one of their enemies in search of prey.

He was Iron Eyes.

The notorious name alone was one which could spread terror throughout an entire community of wanted men once it was uttered. Splintered Rock could have made his fortune if he had started firing his famed Navy Colts in all directions, for it seemed to his knowing eyes that every face he glanced at as he guided his mount along the twisting street belonged to an outlaw with a bounty on his head. Every one of them was wanted, either dead or alive.

Luckily for them Iron Eyes was not hunting any of them. All he wanted was the three brothers who had murdered so many innocent souls across the Pecos.

He would not be distracted by other outlaws, however valuable they were. This no longer had anything to do with the reward money on the Brand brothers' heads. This was now a personal quest to stop them permanently.

The town's main street was filled with more than its share of gambling halls, saloons and whorehouses but that was not what Iron Eyes was seeking. He was looking for a place to rest up and find out where Matt Brand and his siblings were. The town was far bigger than he had expected and he knew that the outlaws he sought could be anywhere within its boundaries.

Then his keen eyes spotted a hotel. He turned the horse and aimed its nose at the wide façade.

Iron Eyes eased back on his reins and stopped his handsome horse beside one of three hitching rails. Without making the slightest noise Iron Eyes raised his right leg over the head and neck of the stallion and slid to the ground.

Then his large spurs rang out a deadly tune as his boots hit the sand.

The bounty hunter led the horse forward to a trough and, as the animal drank, Iron Eyes firmly tied his reins to the long weathered pole.

He ran his bony fingers through his long black hair and felt the sun on his scarred features. He then removed his saddle-bags and hoisted them on to his left shoulder. His eyes darted all about him at the men and women who filled both the street and its boardwalks. None cast their attention back at the tall man who resembled a tortured scarecrow as he slowly stepped up on to the boardwalk. Perhaps all of their eyes were blurred from constant drinking through long endless nights of revelry, he thought. Maybe none of the people in Splintered Rock could actually see anything.

His bony hands adjusted the two guns that poked up from behind his belt buckle. The hideous creature stared all around him.

Satisfied that he had still not been noticed, Iron Eyes turned and entered the open doorway of the hotel. He walked slowly across its bright carpeted lobby towards the long desk and the female who stood reading a newspaper behind it. With each step the spurs jangled as though warning other creatures to keep away from him.

The female looked up.

She saw him.

Her expression altered from happy greeting to one of total shock. She was unable to hide her trepidation even from behind her mask of powder and lip paint. Her entire body was trembling as if she had just seen the Devil himself enter the hotel. Iron Eyes kept walking towards her. His spurs kept jangling.

She opened her mouth to speak but her voice failed to make any noise.

'I want a room,' Iron Eyes mumbled in a low rasping whisper. 'One with a soft bed and a window.'

She was shaking even more uncontrollably.

Unable either to speak or move, every instinct in the female told her to run and hide, but her legs refused to obey. She had seen many men in her life but never anything that resembled the tall man on the other side of the desk. She stared at the gun grips that poked over his belt buckle.

'A room?' she stammered.

Iron Eyes leaned across the desk so their faces were only inches apart. She could smell the whiskey in every word he repeated.

'Yep. I want a room with a real soft bed. Savvy?'

She swallowed hard. Somehow she managed to nod as she tried to control her shaking body. Without speaking she turned and pulled a numbered key from a pigeonhole and dropped it on the thick register before him.

'Much obliged,' the bounty hunter said. He plucked up the key, then turned round and stared out at the bright street. It was as though he was waiting for someone to try their luck and start shooting, but no one did. He remained by the desk looking out at the constant stream of people passing the open doorway. The female turned the book round for him to sign. Her fingers touched his arm.

'You gotta sign the register,' she somehow managed to tell her new guest. 'It's a rule.'

'I didn't know there were any rules in Splintered Rock, ma'am.' The tall man turned back to face her. She started to shake nervously as her eyes focused on the gruesome scars that covered his face. Iron Eyes looked at the pen in its stand, plucked it up and dipped its nib in the inkwell.

She watched him scrawl his name, then he rested the pen on the blotter next to the book.

'Thank you,' she managed to say. 'How long do you think you'll be staying?'

'As long as it takes,' Iron Eyes replied.

'As long as what takes?'

Iron Eyes did not answer. He rammed a fresh cigar between his teeth and produced a match which he struck with a thumbnail. He raised the flame to the long black cigar, inhaled its smoke and then tossed the match into a spittoon. It hissed like a sidewinder.

'I don't reckon there's any law in this town,' the bounty hunter observed. 'Is there?'

She shook her head. 'Nope. There was a couple of locobeans a few years ago who liked wearing tin stars, but they both got themselves shot. Nobody cared for the job after that.'

'Figures.' Iron Eyes sucked in smoke and then blew it at the floor. 'Is there anyone in this hotel able to take my horse to a livery stable? It needs food and water and a brush down.'

She nodded. 'I'll get our porter to see to that.'

Iron Eyes produced a golden eagle and placed it on the register. 'That'll cover it all, I reckon. You keep whatever's left.'

Her eyes widened as she looked at the gleaming fifty-dollar gold piece. 'You could stay for weeks for that much money. Hell.'

Iron Eyes nodded. 'Don't reckon I'll be around that long.'

'You here for a reason?' she asked.

'I'm looking for a few men,' Iron Eyes said through a cloud of smoke. 'The Brand brothers. Have you heard of them?'

'I'm sorry, but I ain't heard of them. Friends of yours?'

'Nope.' Iron Eyes turned towards the impressive staircase.

She shook her head. 'There's a whole lot of folks in town I've never seen before. Sorry I can't help.'

'Don't fret. I'll find them.'

She watched him walk across the lobby and climb the stairs to the upper floor. His spurs kept jangling. As he disappeared from view she turned the book round and then felt her heart skip a beat as she read the name he had written.

'Holy cow!' She gulped as her trembling fingers picked up the gleaming coin. 'Iron Eyes!'

8

Iron Eyes lay fully dressed upon the wide bed, clutching his deadly pair of Navy Colts in his hands. He had only removed his weatherworn trail coat before he lay down upon the soft bedding. He had slept until the sun had set outside his window, yet his eyes had remained open. Every noise from the street had been heard by the bounty hunter, no matter how faint. Just like a wild animal Iron Eyes never truly relaxed for even the briefest of moments. He was fully aware that there was always someone who might try their luck and attempt to kill him. His thin, scar-covered body bore evidence to that simple fact.

He rose up on the bed, dropped his feet to the floor and reattached his sharp spurs to his boots, which he had chosen to keep on his feet. He stood up, moved to the window and stared through the brown lace curtain that covered the four panes of glass. Like an eagle on a high thermal he surveyed the still busy street as his left hand rubbed the rope burns on his sore throat. The amber light which spilled from every doorway and window along the crooked street gave the town an eerie illumination. Innumerable people still filled the street. The sound of many guitars and pianos blended together in a weird symphony of noise which bore no relation to anything that could be called music.

The tall bounty hunter reached down and plucked a bottle of whiskey from his saddle-bags. He raised it to his mouth. His sharp teeth gripped the cork and dragged it free of the glass neck. Iron Eyes spat the cork across the room and started to drink. He glanced at the half-dozen sticks of dynamite he had purchased back in Rio Concho and the coiled fuse wire beside it.

Iron Eyes knew he might have to use every one of the sticks of explosives if things took a turn for the worse in

Splintered Rock. This was a town with too many enemies for his Navy Colts to cope with.

Then, as the fiery whiskey burned its way down into his guts he noticed a group of more than half a dozen well-armed men gathered together in an alley directly across the street from the hotel. They were all staring at the hotel and toying with their gun grips. Iron Eyes placed the bottle down on the floor and strode back to the bed.

His bony hands picked up the pair of guns off the bedding. He rammed them into his pants belt. The cold steel of their long barrels against his flat belly reminded the tall figure that he was no longer asleep but wide awake. He went back towards the window and stared from behind the lace down at the group of men once again.

The men who hid in the shadows might not have been waiting for him but Iron Eyes had lived too long not to recognize trouble when he saw it. Those men were trouble and no mistake.

They must be waiting for him, Iron Eyes thought. He recalled signing the register as he always did. That had been a mistake which might prove to be fatal. The female downstairs must have told someone she had the legendary bounty hunter staying in her hotel. Word spread quickly when the word was about a man who hunted and killed outlaws in a town filled to overflowing with outlaws.

It was dark in his room. That was why he could see them but they could not see him. The men were shuffling around in the alley as if impatient to get on with their evil deed. What other reason could they have to be there? This was a lawless town. The fear of being rounded up by a sheriff did not exist in Splintered Rock. There was no possible reason for anyone to hide in shadows.

Not unless they wanted to get the drop on someone.

'Reckon we'd better get this sorted,' Iron Eyes whispered to himself. 'If I don't go out there it's only a matter of time before they come looking for me here. The odds are better down there.'

Iron Eyes lifted his coat up off the floor. The sound of the pockets filled with loose bullets filled the silent room as he swung its frayed fabric over his shoulders until it rested like a cape. He did not put his arms into the sleeves for some reason that he did not quite understand himself. Something buried deep in his mind told him that it might prove better if he just allowed the old coat to hang over his arms and hands.

He then reached down and picked up one of the dynamite sticks and cut off a six-inch length of fuse wire with the Bowie knife he always kept hidden in his boot neck. He slipped the knife back into the boot and forced the fuse into the top of the explosive. He slid the dynamite into his shirt with the fuse wire exposed near its buttons.

With his arms hidden at his side Iron Eyes turned. He had been in countless tough situations before but he had never found himself in a town filled entirely with outlaws. Not until now.

For a brief moment the bounty hunter wondered if he had bitten off more than even he could chew.

Had he? Only time would tell. He shook off the doubts that had managed to enter his thoughts. He remembered the reason he was here. The trail of the three outlaws he had been tracking for weeks had led him here. Perhaps they were still somewhere within the confines of Splintered Rock. If not he had to discover where they had ridden to. He inhaled deeply.

It took only two strides for the painfully thin legs of the bounty hunter to reach the door. He slid the bolt across, turned its handle and pulled the door towards him. He paused for a moment and listened for any noise out in the dark corridor. There was none.

Iron Eyes stepped into the corridor, locked the door and slipped the key into his pants pocket. He made his way towards the top of the stairs. Every stride was marked by the sound of his bloodstained spurs. The noise echoed all around him off the corridor's wooden walls, but Iron Eyes did not trouble himself that his spurs might warn people of his approach. As always he was ready to kill should anyone make the mistake of trying to end his life.

There would be no emotion. No dread or doubt.

If someone shot at him he would punish them lethally.

His eyes burned down from the landing. The female was no longer behind the desk down in the lobby. An old man who looked closer to death than birth was seated in a hard chair. The sound of his snoring resonated around the hotel. Iron Eyes slowly descended the stairs with his trail coat draped over his broad bony shoulders. The breeze from the open doorway lifted the frayed tails of his bloodstained coat as he reached the lobby.

Iron Eyes stopped.

Three carefully positioned oil lamps lit up the area around him. His eyes darted around the large room until he was satisfied that there was no one hidden anywhere. He started to walk again. The sound of his spurs rivalled the snoring of the frail old man as Iron Eyes walked towards the open doorway. The amber-lit darkness was in total contrast to the brightly illuminated hotel, yet his eyes adjusted swiftly.

He was still thinking of the men he had seen opposite the hotel. Even though he knew that they might be waiting to ambush him Iron Eyes did not slow his pace. He did not want anyone to think that he was afraid, because he was not.

Iron Eyes stepped out on to the boardwalk and rested his back against the wall next to the open doorway. The porch above his head cast enough shadow to conceal him from anyone trying to get him in their gun sights. It also allowed him to observe them more clearly.

He could tell that they had spotted him walk from the brightly lit lobby and that now they were unsure where he was. The men were starting to break cover as they tried to work out where he had gone.

Crowds of men and women were still filling the boardwalks as they readied themselves for the long night ahead. They moved past Iron Eyes in both directions in a constant stream. None seemed to notice the gaunt bounty hunter leaning against the wooden wall of the hotel.

The street between the bounty hunter and the alley was still busy as horsemen rode up and down its length. There was a steady noise which came from every one of the saloons to either side. Voices of men and women mixed with various musical instruments created a cacophanous din.

Iron Eyes stretched up to his full height and looked over the heads of the people who continued to walk by him. He squinted hard and watched the gunmen fan out. He counted them and then nodded to himself. He would need both his guns if the heavily armed men tried their luck, he thought.

There were seven in total.

The starlight danced on their guns. They had a lot of them and Iron Eyes reasoned that every one of their bullets was intended for him. Then he noticed that their weaponry was no longer holstered. They were drawn and ready to be used.

The bounty hunter lowered his head.

Iron Eyes knew he had been right from the first moment he had spied them. They were going to attempt to kill him because he was the most dangerous thing any outlaw could ever face. He was a man who made his living by killing wanted outlaws for the reward money on their heads.

If there was going to be a showdown it would be on his terms. He would find the place that offered him the best chance of survival. Iron Eyes glanced at the still busy street and boardwalks. A wry smile crept over his horrific features. He knew that even here in a totally lawless town the seven gunmen would probably not open fire until they had a clear target.

There were far too many people between their weaponry and his tall frame. Too many innocent targets. If any should happen to get caught in the crossfire of an ambush the wrath of Splintered Rock would certainly be brought down upon the gunmen.

Iron Eyes grinned.

This was a game he had played before.

He produced a cigar from an inside coat pocket, gripped it between his teeth and stepped away from the hotel wall. He joined the crowd of townsfolk walking past the hotel. He struck a match with his thumbnail and raised its flickering flame to the cigar. He inhaled the smoke and glanced over his shoulder. They had spotted him and were following.

Within eight strides he had reached a saloon and entered its smoky interior. There was no faltering in his approach to the crowded bar. He glanced around at the crowd of men and women who filled the long room as a bartender cautiously approached him.

'Whiskey,' Iron Eyes said, tossing a couple of coins at the silent man behind the wet counter. 'A bottle.'

The bartender caught the coins and placed a bottle in front of the bounty hunter. He remained silent as his smoke-filled eyes focused on the scarred face of his customer.

Iron Eyes walked away from the counter and strode through the crowd until he reached a table and chair set at the very end of the room. A drunken man sat on the chair, drinking beer and dribbling on the table. The man looked up at the horrific face of the bounty hunter. He gasped. Even a day of drinking could not make the sight of Iron Eyes accept-able even to a drunkard.

'I'd move if I was you,' Iron Eyes said.

'Why should I?' the drunken man asked.

'There's gonna be a whole lot of bullets heading in this direction mighty soon, friend,' Iron Eyes told him. 'Stay there if ya want to get yourself killed.'

The drunken man heeded the warning. He downed what was remaining of his beer, then scrambled to his feet and kept on walking until he was no longer in the saloon but headed for a safer haven. The sound of the tinny piano less than ten feet away from Iron Eyes drew the attention of the bounty hunter. The piano player either had very fat fingers or he was simply far too drunk to attempt any musical reditions, Iron Eyes thought before picking up the empty beer glass.

Glazed eyes glanced at the towering bounty hunter as the self-appointed pianist continued to thrash the black and white keys of the piano.

'What'll it be, handsome?' the man asked. 'You name a tune and I'll play it for the price of a beer.'

'I'd like you to quit playing,' Iron Eyes said.

'Sorry. I don't quit until bedtime.'

'Sweet dreams.' Iron Eyes shielded his action from the rest of the saloon bar as he brought the hefty glass down across the man's skull. The glass remained intact as the piano player slumped forward. No one noticed the blood which was trickling from the wound that spanned his head. Iron Eyes placed the blood-covered beer glass on top of the upright piano next to a dozen others and then turned back to the table.

Iron Eyes placed the whiskey bottle down, then seated himself with his back to the wall. He screwed up his eyes and stared across the long room at the swing doors. There were at least fifty men and women between himself and the entrance to the saloon. A cloud of tobacco smoke hung about four feet above the sawdust-covered floor.

He puffed on the cigar and waited. He did not have to wait long. Before he had time to pull the cork from the bottle he saw the heads of seven men looking over the top of the swing doors. Iron Eyes removed the cork and then withdrew an old crumpled Wanted poster from his coat pocket. He rolled the paper up and poked it into the neck of the clear glass bottle. He watched as the paper absorbed the whiskey.

'That'll do.' He smiled.

Defiantly Iron Eyes rose so that they could see him through the lingering smoke that hung in the stale air of the saloon. His teeth gripped the cigar tightly. The seven men saw him and pushed their way into the crowded bar. Even though not one word was spoken every one of the saloon's patrons realized what was about to occur.

In a few seconds every one of the men and women had left the saloon. Even the bartender had taken flight. Now there were only the seven gunmen and the impassive bounty hunter remaining in the saloon.

The seven men started casting tables and chairs aside as they moved steadily towards the motionless Iron Eyes.

'Are you Iron Eyes?' one of their number yelled out, waving his six-shooter as though it were a fan.

For a moment Iron Eyes did not reply. He simply pulled the cigar from his lips and touched the whiskey-sodden paper, which still poked out from the bottle's neck. A flame two feet high flared upwards. Then, faster than the blink of an eye, the bounty hunter grabbed the bottle off the table and hurled it at the group of approaching gunmen. The tobacco smoke had blinded them to what was happening until it was too late.

A heartbeat before the bottle reached its targets Iron Eyes drew one of his Navy Colts and fanned its hammer. His bullet hit the glass projectile. Burning whiskey engulfed the seven gunmen. Each of them erupted into flame as the fiery whiskey turned them into fireballs. The men's haunting screams filled the saloon as they all crashed into one another as well as the saloon walls in a futile attempt to escape.

Their guns blasted in all directions as the grim-faced bounty hunter watched the flames race across the sawdust-covered floor and then spread unchecked up the walls of the saloon. The human torches tried desperately not only to extinguish the flames that had engulfed them, but also to kill the bounty hunter. Both attempts were doomed to failure. As the gunmen began to blacken the bounty hunter drew his second gun. His bony thumbs pulled both weapons' hammers back until they locked. Then he fired. He repeated the action until he had dispatched all seven of his adversaries to their Maker.

The saloon was now engulfed in flame.

It was impossible to see the front of the building and its swing doors from where the tall figure stood holding his deadly Colts. A wall of raging fire was consuming everything like a voracious monster unable to satisfy itself.

Iron Eyes turned and walked to the table again as bottles of whiskey stacked behind the bar counter started to explode and add even more fuel to the inferno.

The tall man patted the dynamite stick still in his shirt. He had not yet been forced to use it but he was convinced he would have to before the night grew much older.

There was a door set close to the piano. Iron Eyes turned its handle and walked out into the dark alley. As the cold air raced through the open doorway he heard even more explosions inside the doomed saloon.

He had only one regret. So much whiskey had been wasted.

Iron Eyes moved through the alley until he was back on the main street's boardwalk. The crowd was ten deep and growing. It seemed that fire had a way of drawing people towards it like ancient sirens beckoning unsuspecting seafarers. Iron Eyes strode back in the direction of the hotel and heard his name mentioned several times. It seemed that every one of the townsfolk believed that he had also been consumed by the fire.

A wry smile carved across his face.

Then he saw the drunken man he had stolen the table and chair from back in the saloon. The man was barely conscious but still determined to have a good time. He was seated on the edge of a trough, watching the flames rise up into the night sky.

Iron Eyes stood before the man. He waited until the baggy eyes looked up at him before he spoke.

'You know the Brand brothers?' Iron Eyes asked.

The man gave a firm nod. 'I do. Me and Matt go way back.'

'Where are they?'

The man considered the question, then nodded again as he recalled the answer. 'They lit out with their pa and headed up to the forest. Why'd ya wanna know?'

'Why'd they head there?' the bounty hunter pressed.

The man tapped the side of his nose and closed one eye in a pathetic attempt to wink. 'Wouldn't you like to know?'

Angrily Iron Eyes grabbed the man

by the head and hauled him backwards. The water in the trough overflowed its wooden sides as Iron Eyes submerged the drunkard. Only when the bubbles stopped rising from the water did Iron Eyes drag the man back up and allow him to suck in air.

'Answer my damn question,' Iron Eyes rasped.

'Curley Jake said he'd found gold,' the drunk spluttered.

Iron Eyes was confused. 'But them boys had themselves a whole heap of gold.'

The drunkard sat in the trough and wagged a finger at the ominous figure above him. 'Not gold coin. Curley found a whole cave of real gold. Found it growing there.'

'Where is this forest?' the bounty hunter asked as he watched the flames of the saloon engulf the buildings to either side of it. 'Which way do I head?'

The drunken man raised a hand out of the water and pointed over his shoulder.

'Thataway. Ya can't miss it. It's covered in trees.'

Having learned where the deadly Brand brothers had headed Iron Eyes marched back to his hotel to get his saddle-bags. He would then go to the livery stables and get his horse.

The hunt was back on.

9

A million stars set against a sky of black velvet sparkled like precious jewels above the lone horseman as he drove his powerful mount ever onward. Iron Eyes had not taken long to pick up the hoof tracks of the three Brand brothers and their father's mounts once he had ridden from Splintered Rock. All he had required was for someone to aim a finger in the right direction and the drunken man had done just that.

Fuelled by cigars and whiskey Iron Eyes continued his relentless quest across the vast prairie towards the dark forested hills. It was nearly three hours since he had mounted the magnificent stallion and spurred away but, even now as he looked back, he could still see the raging inferno he had created.

The whiskey-fuelled fire had spread throughout the outlaws' town quickly.

Tinder-dry wooden structures built far too close to one another created an accident waiting to happen.

The accident had a name and it was Iron Eyes.

Now he could smell the forest. He inhaled its aroma and recalled his earlier days. Days when he was just like the animals that roamed free over the land. Every creature had its chosen prey and only the fittest survived. That was where he had learned everything he knew about hunting.

The deadly outlaws had no way of knowing that, although they had tried, they had failed to kill him. They were now his prey. Soon he would prove who was the fittest.

Soon Iron Eyes would get his revenge. Not for what they had done to him, but for what they had done back at Rio Concho.

There would be no mercy. Their breed did not deserve it.

Dead or alive meant only one thing to Iron Eyes. It meant dead. There were no alternatives. The Brand brothers had chosen their own destiny when they had turned from bank robbers to mindless killers of innocent souls.

Iron Eyes would be their judge, jury and executioner.

The haunting sounds of wild animals as they bayed to the moonlit sky filled the dry air as the tireless stallion thundered towards the forest. Iron Eyes paid them no heed. He had heard the painful cries far too many times before. It was as though every animal in the forest sensed the danger that was heading towards them. Maybe it was the scent of death, which the rider had never been able to shake off his flesh and clothing, that the creatures detected.

Whatever it was that alarmed them they knew there was nothing they could do to stop his progress. Iron Eyes was coming. His long black hair floated over his broad shoulders and beat its steady rhythm as he headed towards them.

Death always rode with the bounty hunter. It was his constant companion.

The acrid aroma of countless killings lingered on every part of his emaciated form. Every pore of his body oozed with the putrid memory of death. It clung to him like a second skin. Every one of his countless victims had somehow marked him with their own scent.

It was the scent of death itself.

Sensing that soon he would enter the dark forest, Iron Eyes drove his spurs into the stallion even harder. The horse responded and increased its pace.

The calls of the alarmed creatures far ahead of the deadly rider grew more intense. His eyes narrowed and focused on the trail of the four horsemen he had followed for nearly half the long night. He could see where they had entered the forest and knew that they were now closer than they had been since he had battled with them back at Anvil City.

Soon he would be in the forest. Soon he would be able to use every one of his honed skills to capture and kill them. There was no escape from someone like the bounty hunter, for he had grown to manhood in a forest similar to the one he was now approaching. He would become the most dangerous animal within its boundaries again. The trees and the bushes were his to read. There had never been a trail he could not follow as clearly as though it were the text of a book.

There was no more dangerous animal than the one known as Iron Eyes. Soon he would prove that fact to the Brand brothers.

With each long stride of his horse mighty Iron Eyes kept remembering the face of the young girl back at Rio Concho. A dead face that haunted him. There would only be one way to put her memory to rest and that was to avenge her death.

Feeling the palomino beginning to flag beneath him Iron Eyes pulled back on his reins and stopped the weary horse. The bounty hunter stared ahead of him across the moonlit sand to where a wall of tall trees covered the rolling hillside.

His eyes vainly searched for a campfire. They must have made camp by now, he reasoned. Even the deadliest of outlaws slept. Or maybe they had been taken to the mysterious cave of gold by their father.

Yet no matter how hard Iron Eyes looked at the wall of trees he could not see any light from a fire which could have betrayed their position.

A thought occurred to him. What if they had spotted him trailing them? What if they were waiting for him? Waiting to bushwhack him before he could get the better of them?

A smile crossed his hardened features.

They could try, he mused. They could try.

He inhaled the night air deeply and then tapped the dynamite stick, which he still had tucked in his shirt. It was cold against his bare belly. A constant reminder that he had not needed to use it back at Splintered Rock.

His hunter's instinct told him that his

prey was close. He could smell them on the night air. Their scent filled his flared nostrils.

Reluctantly Iron Eyes swung a long lean leg over the head of his huge mount and slid to the ground.

Iron Eyes unhooked a rusting tin bowl from his saddle and placed it on the sand in front of the palomino. He hauled one of his canteens from the saddle horn, unscrewed its stopper and filled the bowl with the precious liquid. The skeletal figure continued to stare in vain with icy determination towards the forest for any hint of a campfire casting its flickering light through the trees.

There still was no sign of a camp.

While the horse drank, Iron Eyes replaced the canteen next to others and checked the remaining sticks of dynamite in his saddle-bags. He had never used explosives before, but something deep in his craw told him that this hunt was different from all previous ones.

The Brand brothers were vermin, but they had already bettered him once. He knew they worked together as though they were one person and not three. Some kin were able to do that, he had once been told. It was as if each knew what the others would do even before they did it.

They were dangerous.

Far more dangerous than their Wanted poster implied.

His entire concentration was focused on the forest and the three outlaws who, he knew, were now almost within his grasp.

'Ya all dead men,' Iron Eyes growled. 'Ya just don't know it yet.'

The horse finished drinking. Iron Eyes scooped the bowl up and reattached it to the saddle just behind the cantle. Then he reached up, grabbed the saddle horn and hoisted himself in to the saddle. He collected the reins up in his bony hands.

He glanced at the heavens and gave a satisfied nod to himself. The moon had set now; its light would not betray his steady approach, he thought. There was only the faint illumination of a multitude of stars scattered across a cloudy sky.

'Perfect,' he whispered.

The bounty hunter looked back again and saw distant flames rising up into the heavens. Splintered Rock was still ablaze. Then, just as he turned to face the forest he spotted a dim light set somewhere in the trees.

At first he thought he had spied the campfire he had been searching for. Then it became obvious that the light he saw was moving through the trees.

'A torch,' Iron Eyes said knowingly.

They were riding along a trail halfway up the forested hillside. Iron Eyes jerked the stallion's head up from the sand, where it had been licking the spilled droplets of water. He leaned forward and encouraged it towards the flickering light of the distant torch.

'C'mon,' he said, and spurred.

The stallion exploded into action and galloped ahead.

10

There was an eerie silence as the bounty hunter entered the forest. The fearful howling that had greeted his approach suddenly stopped. Iron Eyes neither noticed nor cared, for he had other things now to concentrate on. He reined in and the sturdy horse snorted as its master rose up in his stirrups and stared into the gloom. The four men were on foot. The bounty hunter could just make them out through the trees far above him as one of them carried the fiery torch and led the others ever upward.

They were at least a hundred feet higher up the hillside than the watching horseman. Iron Eyes wondered whether the story he had been told by the drunkard might just be true.

Were they actually going to a cave filled with golden ore?

Could there be such a place?

Iron Eyes looked around him and then spied a line of horses standing at the edge of the forest. He dragged his reins around and rode to them. There were four saddle horses and half a dozen pack mules. All of them were tethered in what the bounty hunter could only assume must be a crude campsite.

Iron Eyes dismounted and walked to the first three of the horses. They still had the canvas bags of gold coin across their necks. The tall bounty hunter was confused.

Why would the Brand brothers be interested in coming here with their father? They already had a fortune in gold hanging on either side of their horses' shoulders.

Would golden ore and precious nuggets arouse the same lust in them? It did not make any sense to the bounty hunter as he tied the reins of his own mount to a tree trunk and looked back up at the high trail along which the men were still moving. They had stolen enough money back at Rio Concho to last them their entire lifetimes, he thought.

Then he remembered what somebody had once told him. For some men there was no such thing as enough money. Whether gold, silver or simply paper money, some greedy men could never be satisfied. They always wanted more.

Iron Eyes dragged his saddle-bags off the stallion's back and lowered them on to the dark ground. As always the satchels were filled with oats, whiskey bottles and boxes of ammunition, but this time he had brought six sticks of dynamite as well. Five sticks in a satchel and the sixth tucked inside his shirt. Each of them now sported a short fuse and only needed a naked flame or the touch of a glowing cigar tip to ignite them.

The gaunt figure rubbed his scarred neck with the palm of his hand and wondered whether he would actually require the deadly explosives. So far his keen-witted cunning had been enough. He lifted one of the whiskey bottles and pulled its cork with his sharp teeth. He spat the cork away and started to drink. Nearly half the bottle's fiery contents burned down into his guts before he lowered it and snorted.

His throat still hurt badly. It was a constant reminder that three of the men above him on the narrow trail had hanged him.

He finished what was left of the whiskey and stared up with avenging eyes. The torchlight danced off the moving Brand brothers as they continued to trek between the trees towards their goal.

Iron Eyes considered the situation. He did not want to underestimate Matt Brand or his brothers again. That arrogance had almost cost him his life. This time he had to do it right and defeat them.

Yet they were a tricky bunch. Far trickier than most of the vermin he had hunted over the previous few years. It was as though they actually believed that they were invulnerable.

Was it the luck of the insane that protected them? Or was it that they were better than most men in their profession? If you killed everyone who had witnessed your crimes it ensured that there would be very few men brave enough to trail you afterwards. Whatever it was that drove the Brand brothers to commit their ruthless atrocities, there was no question that it worked.

Iron Eyes had nearly had his neck snapped when he had tackled them. They might be totally insane, he thought, but the Brand brothers were still unscathed. He bore the scars of his brutal encounter with them.

Iron Eyes reached down and grabbed the primed sticks of dynamite. He stuffed them deep into his trail-coat pockets next to the scores of loose bullets, then he straightened up to his full height.

He looked upward at the sky.

There was an ominous hue across its

expanse. One by one the stars were fading. Dawn was coming, he silently acknowledged. He would have to move quickly if he were to use what was left of nightfall to help him get the better of his foes.

Iron Eyes returned his attention to the woodland and knew that this was the terrain that suited him best. The forest made him feel confident. He knew how to move swiftly through muddy ground and between countless trees. Move unseen by whatever he was hunting. Few men could have equalled the agility or speed the thin figure possessed when in a forest.

Unlike the four men ahead of him Iron Eyes would not use the narrow mountain trail. There was a far quicker way to ascend the steep hillside. He took a more direct route to where he had last seen the flaming torch.

Like a puma the surefooted Iron Eyes raced up the slippery tree-lined slope. He used every tree and sapling to his advantage. He grabbed hold of them in the confident knowledge that they would support his weight as he propelled himself further and further up the steep incline.

Iron Eyes had chosen a direct course that he knew would bring him out ahead of the four more cautious men on the winding trail. His honed instincts told him exactly where the Brand brothers and their father were headed. Iron Eyes was determined to get there before them.

Hidden by the darkness that some might have considered a hindrance Iron Eyes made it to his goal unseen. He reached the muddy level ground of the pathway and knelt down. His eyes squinted through the gloom back along the trail as he waited for his prey. Hundreds of trees of every size and shape stood proudly between the bounty hunter and the four men he knew would soon come round the perilous corner and face him. He had no interest in the man who, he had been informed, was their father. His war was with Matt Brand and his siblings and it was a fight he was more than ready for. Iron Eyes drew one of his guns, cocked its hammer and waited.

The light of the torch danced on the tree trunks as the four men got closer to where Iron Eyes knelt. Then to the bounty hunter's surprise the flickering light of the torch disappeared from view.

Iron Eyes rose from his knees and crouched low with his gun aimed straight ahead of him. His eyes burned through the darkness. A million thoughts and considerations filled his mind. Had they spotted him clambering up the slope? Had they extinguished the torch so that they could once again get the better of him?

Slowly he stretched his long lean form until he was standing tall. There had been no hint that they knew they were not alone on the tree-covered hillside, he thought. There was another reason why the torchlight had vanished. There had to be.

Like a monstrous creature from the bowels of Hell itself the hideous bounty hunter started to move through the shadows towards the corner. Each step rang out with the sound of his large spurs. He knew that the noise of his bloody spurs might betray him, but it might also make the curious step away from cover.

All he needed was a target to shoot at. Then he would prove once and for all that the Brand brothers were not invincible and could die as easily as anyone else.

Then Iron Eyes had another thought: they had reached the cave and entered it. That must be why he could no longer see any sign of torchlight. They had entered the cave.

The slippery pathway led around the very edge of the steep hillside. Countless trees rose from the fertile soil both above and below it. Iron Eyes reached the corner and looked around from behind a tree trunk that was wider than he was. His eyes searched the dark foliage to his left. For a moment he was confused. There seemed to be no sign of a cave and there was no sign of any of the Brands either.

They had vanished off the side of the mountain. Iron Eyes ventured forward along the slim trail and stared at the brush that draped down between the trees. At first glance it seemed solid, then the torchlight filtered through the dense screen of greenery before him.

It told him where his enemies were.

Once again Iron Eyes moved with the speed and agility of a mountain cat. He raced to the hanging vines of ivy, then paused. The light of a torch from inside the cave penetrated the thick vines and animated the otherwise emotionless face.

Iron Eyes pulled the tangled growth apart to reveal the entrance to the cave. The torch had been forced into the soft floor of the cave. Its yard-high flame rose from the coal-tar-soaked rags that had been wrapped around its tip. The flaming light was multiplied a hundred times as it reflected off the walls of the twenty-foot-high cave. Iron Eyes was seldom impressed by anything but he felt himself gasp in awe as he stared open-mouthed at the walls of the cave.

They were indeed made of golden rock.

The light was blinding in its intensity.

To the bounty hunter it was as if he had discovered an ancient wonder. Iron Eyes lowered his head and shielded his eyes with his free hand as he kept a firm grip on the Navy Colt in the other. He walked forward into the cave in search of the wanted men as his eyes adjusted to the blinding light. He stopped.

To his utter surprise he was looking down upon the body of the old prospector lying on the cave floor just beyond the flaming torch. A pool of fresh blood encircled Curley Jake's head.

The bounty hunter frowned. Had the Brand brothers killed their own father? The question screamed inside his head. The answer was obvious. Iron Eyes stooped and removed his spurs and left them on the ground next to the body of Curley Jake.

Iron Eyes rose to his feet and plucked the torch from the ground. He turned it upside down and rammed its flame into the damp soil. Blackness enveloped the fearless bounty hunter. Now the only light inside the cave was coming from an unseen torch deeper in the cavernous tunnel. A wall of rock jutted out making a corner that divided the golden cave into two sections.

His mind vainly tried to understand why sons would kill their father. Were there no depths of depravity these three deadly killers would not sink to? The old man had proudly brought his sons to show them his discovery and they had repaid him by slitting his throat.

Then Iron Eyes heard jovial voices of men just out of sight around the glistening wall of the cavern, twenty feet ahead of him. The light of the other torch cast the shadows of three men on the golden walls.

Then he heard them laughing.

Iron Eyes had those laughing voices carved into his memory. It was the

same mocking laughter as he had last
heard when the noose had been tightened around his scrawny neck and they'd
hoisted him up off the ground.

The skeletal figure moved through
the darkness silently towards the sound
of their gut-wrenching voices. Every
inch of him wanted to kill them now,
but he knew that however insane they
were they had a way of eluding his
bullets. The had a way of turning the
tables on him.

Iron Eyes stopped walking. His eyes
watched their shadows on the glistening
wall of gold to his left. He readied
himself and then bellowed.

'Brand. I've come to kill you, boys.'
His words echoed off the cave's walls.
He watched their shadows and lowered
his gun until it was level with his hip.
His finger stroked the trigger.

Matt Brand called back. 'And who
the hell might you be?'

'Iron Eyes.'

'Then prepare to die, Iron Eyes,' the
eldest of the Brand boys answered. 'Me

and my brothers don't cotton to folks putting their noses in our business.'

'I see you already killed your pa, boys,' Iron Eyes yelled out. 'How come?'

Matt Brand was the only one of the three with the wits to answer the question. His voice snarled out its spitting reply,

'We don't need him no more. That's why.'

Iron Eyes continued to watch their shadows as they traced across the glistening cave wall. He tried to work out where exactly the men were beyond the golden cave wall but it was impossible. Flickering torchlight confused the tall bounty hunter. If he were to believe the shadowy images before him, the Brand brothers were twenty feet tall. Iron Eyes knew that there was only one way to end this stand-off.

There had to be a face-to-face showdown.

Nothing less would resolve this, he thought. Iron Eyes rubbed his raw neck and thought about the small child back in Rio Concho. He could still feel her cold skin on his fingertips.

They had to pay for that monstrous act. Pay with their putrid hides. Nothing else would satisfy the avenging bounty hunter. The Brand brothers and Iron Eyes had to face one another with guns blazing. He had to lure them out from the back of the cave.

An idea suddenly came to him. 'Reckon I'll leave you boys back there and use a few sticks of dynamite to block the entrance to this cave. Reckon you'll all rot in here but you'll be real wealthy corpses, thanks to your pa.'

The voice of Matt Brand called out. 'I'd not try doing that if I was you, Iron Eyes.'

Iron Eyes could hear the concern in Brand's voice. 'This is my game, Brand. I hold all the best cards. There's only one way you can stop me but I figure that none of you got the guts to even try.'

'Ain't we?'

'Nope.' Iron Eyes moved across the

sand towards the dead body. 'Then I'll take all that gold coin you got hanging on your horses. Reckon I'm the only winner in this game. Gotta thank you all, though, for doing all the hard work for me.'

The bounty hunter stopped as the back of the cave was also plunged into darkness. They had snuffed out their torch just as he had done with the one next to the dead man. The length of the cave was in total darkness.

Iron Eyes was facing the back of the cave with his Navy Colt still firmly gripped in his bony hand. He listened hard and heard the movement of their spurs.

'Hope ya can see in the dark, Iron Eyes,' Matt Brand called out loudly. 'Me and my kin are coming to kill ya.'

Unafraid, Iron Eyes lowered his head and raised his gun. Then he heard them running towards him. Their weapons started to blast lethal lead just as he had hoped they would.

11

The noise of the outlaws' guns was magnified inside the cave a hundredfold. Shafts of red-hot tapers came from their gun barrels as the cave reverberated with the deafening sound of continuous gunfire. Their bullets tore through the long tails of Iron Eyes' trail coat, but he did not move. He could feel the heat of their lead as bullets passed close to his thin tall frame. Too close.

A lesser man might have sought cover but not the bounty hunter. Iron Eyes felt their bullets tear across his flesh as the three men continued to fire, coming closer and closer to their target.

Then a strange unearthly noise filled the cave as the Brand brothers continued to shoot blindly in search of the bounty hunter. It sounded as though a giant was stirring above their heads. The entire cave started to shake as more and more shots rang out their ear-splitting cadences.

The roof of the cave groaned. Unseen cracks spread across it. Dust began to fall like rain. Then small stones, followed by larger ones fell all across the cavern. The ancient golden rocks that spanned the ceiling of the cave were unable to withstand the deafening reverberation and hold firm. More rocks started to fall around the four men.

When the Brand brothers got to within ten feet of the stationary Iron Eyes the deadly bounty hunter fanned his gun hammer over and over again until the Navy Colt's chambers were empty.

With each flash from his smoking gun barrel Iron Eyes had seen the notorious outlaws fall one after another. They lay in a bloody heap at his feet as he switched guns. Then Iron Eyes heard one of the brothers groaning in the smoke-filled blackness. Coldly, Iron Eyes aimed and fired his weapon down at the noise.

The outlaw fell silent.

With the echoes of the brief battle still bouncing off the cave walls a noise Iron Eyes had never heard before filled him with dread. He knew that the roof of gold above him was about to collapse.

Iron Eyes walked over the dead outlaws' bodies and then answered Matt Brand's earlier question. 'Yep. I can see in the dark, Brand.'

Just as he was about to head towards the cave's opening he heard a mighty cracking sound. It raced across the roof of the cave high over his head. The bounty hunter looked upward and then heard an even more troubling sound.

Tons of golden rock suddenly crashed down all around the stunned figure. Boulders sent choking dust in all directions in the darkness. It was as though the whole hillside was imploding upon itself. Desperately Iron Eyes threw himself against the wall of the cave. He scrambled as close to it as his lean form could manage. The roof fall seemed to go on for ever.

At last the deadly rockfall ended. Only choking dust remained, hanging in the air. The dazed bounty hunter pushed the debris off his bruised legs and scrambled back to his feet.

Blindly, he staggered over the mass of rocks until he found the torch next to the body of the old prospector. He dragged it out of the ground and pulled a match from his pocket. He lit the oil rags wrapped around its tip, then rammed it between some of the rocks. His dust-filled eyes surveyed the torchlit chaos which faced him.

'This ain't good. Ain't good at all,' Iron Eyes said. His eyes focused on the dead bodies of the Brand brothers. They were half-buried by tons of huge rocks, which were piled up to where the cave entrance had been only moments previously. Iron Eyes made his way back towards the massive pile of golden rocks, which had completely blocked the mouth of the cave. He rested his bony hands upon the rocks, stared at the debris and then shook his head.

He was trapped.

Iron Eyes was entombed.

Finale

The battered stagecoach had travelled throughout the night and had arrived at the edge of the forest a couple of hours after sunrise. Squirrel Sally brought her team to a halt and leapt down to the ground with her trusty Winchester in her hands. She entered the forest and followed the tracks to where the palomino stallion was tethered, close to the other horses and mules. She was about to call out when a mighty explosion sent a fireball shooting out from the hillside above her.

Sally ducked and stared wide-eyed as the flames turned to black smoke and rose up into the cloudless blue sky above the forest.

'What in tarnation was that?' the female blurted out as she watched smoking debris rain down over the trees.

Shock waves from the explosion washed over her. She raced up the slope and then saw a figure emerge from the cave. It was Iron Eyes. He looked more dead than alive as he descended the steep incline towards her. His narrowed eyes glanced at the young female.

'So you found me, huh?' he quipped as he reached his palomino. His bloody hands pulled a bottle from the saddle-bag and were about to raise the whiskey to his mouth when Sally intercepted the bottle. She took a long swallow, then handed it back to the forlorn figure.

'Did ya just blow up that mountain?' she asked.

He lowered the bottle from his lips and swallowed the whiskey. 'I sure did, Squirrel.'

'Why?'

'Why? It was the only way I could get out of that damn cave.' Iron Eyes took another long swig. 'I was trapped in there. The roof of the cave fell in on me.'

Squirrel Sally scrunched up her

handsome features and glared at the man who towered over her. 'How'd ya do it?'

'Dynamite.' Iron Eyes handed the bottle back to her and then found a cigar in his saddle-bags. He placed it between his teeth, struck a match and lit it. His lungs were grateful for the acrid smoke that filled them. 'Trouble is, I used too much. Ain't nothing left of the outlaws I shot. They got blown to bits up there.'

'How many sticks did ya use?'

'Six.' Iron Eyes placed his head against his saddle. It was cold and felt good. 'Reckon one stick would have done it, though.'

Sally moved closer to him and placed her head against his blackened coat sleeve. 'As long as ya OK, sweetheart. That's all that matters. Now we can find us a preacher and get hitched.'

The bounty hunter looked down at her. 'Why would we wanna do that, Squirrel? You hardly know me and I ain't even sure I like you.'

'We're betrothed, ain't we?' she asked.

He shook his head. 'Nope. We ain't.'

'Yes we are,' she argued. 'Ya touched my chest and that means ya gotta marry me. It's the law.'

'As I recall you shot me and I was blind at the time, Squirrel.' Iron Eyes inhaled on his cigar. 'That don't mean we're betrothed. Just means I'm damn unlucky.'

Sally frowned. She paced around the tall Iron Eyes as he checked all his cuts and grazes. It did not seem possible but he looked in even worse shape than usual. The bounty hunter glanced at her.

'How'd you get here, Squirrel?' Iron Eyes looked out at the prairie and the smoke which was still rising from the distant Splintered Rock. 'And how'd you get past that town down yonder without being shot?'

She wrapped herself around him. 'Ain't much of a town any more. Half of it is still on fire. Ya wouldn't happen to know who started that fire, would ya?'

Iron Eyes took the bottle from her small hands and lifted it back to his mouth. As he swallowed its fiery contents she noticed the fresh scars on his neck.

'How'd ya do that?' She poked at the red scarred flesh.

He lowered the bottle. 'I got myself hung.'

Squirrel looked puzzled, then remembered the encounter she had had with the one-armed man. 'Oh yeah. There's a one-armed varmint named Wolfe looking for ya, darling.'

Iron Eyes looked down at her. 'Did he say his name was Wolfe with an e?'

'Yeah, whatever that means.' Squirrel Sally nodded. 'Ya know him? Is he a pal of yours?'

'That's hard to say.' The bounty hunter shrugged. 'We ain't locked horns for a long time. The last time we did he got real ornery with me.'

'How come?' Sally was curious.

'I kinda shot his arm off by mistake,' the bounty hunter admitted. 'Some folks hold a grudge over things like that.'

She watched Iron Eyes as he gathered together the reins of the three horses laden down with gold coin and tied them to his own saddle fender. 'What was ya doing up in a cave anyway?'

'Trying to collect bounty and keep a promise to a little dead gal, Squirrel.' Iron Eyes sighed. 'Reckon I used too much dynamite to collect the reward, but we might get a few bucks for returning the bank's gold coin, though.'

Sally was trailing him towards her stagecoach but thinking about the cave. 'I still don't figure on why ya ended up in a dumb cave, Iron Eyes.'

'It sure weren't no ordinary cave, Squirrel,' the bounty hunter said. 'It was a cave with walls of solid gold.'

She raised a disbelieving eyebrow. 'Ain't no such thing.'

Iron Eyes glanced up at the hillside and the smoke which still billowed from the destruction he had caused with his dynamite. 'Not any more.'

'Ya just joshing with me, ain't ya?' Sally grabbed hold of him, slid her petite hand into his pants pocket and felt a bulge. She smiled excitedly. 'My, what have we here?'

The tall man watched as she pulled out a gleaming golden nugget from his pocket. Her jaw dropped.

'This is gold, darling.'

Iron Eyes nodded. He led the horses to the stagecoach tailgate and secured them. 'It sure is. It must have got in my pocket when the cave roof fell in on me. Keep it.'

He walked to the front of the stage. She followed with her rifle in one hand and the gold nugget in the other. Iron Eyes paused.

'Ya fretting about that Wolfe fella?' Sally asked.

'Nope.' Iron Eyes climbed up to the driver's seat and took hold of the hefty reins. She clambered up beside him, rested her head against his shoulder and purred. Then she dropped her rifle and forced her fingers back into his pants pocket. 'Ya looking for more gold nuggets, Squirrel?'

'Nope.' Sally grinned mischievously. His bony fingers touched her cheek and then he nodded. She was warm, he thought. He liked that.

'Let's see how much reward money they'll pay us for returning this gold coin.' Iron Eyes released the brake and slapped the reins down on the team of lathered up horses. The stagecoach pulled away from the forest. It would not stop again until it reached Rio Concho.

THE END

We do hope that you have enjoyed
reading this large print book.

Did you know that all of our titles
are available for purchase?

We publish a wide range of high
quality large print books including:
Romances, Mysteries, Classics
General Fiction
Non Fiction and Westerns

Special interest titles available in
large print are:
The Little Oxford Dictionary
Music Book, Song Book
Hymn Book, Service Book

Also available from us courtesy of
Oxford University Press:
Young Readers' Dictionary
(large print edition)
Young Readers' Thesaurus
(large print edition)

For further information or a free
brochure, please contact us at:
Ulverscroft Large Print Books Ltd.,
The Green, Bradgate Road, Anstey,
Leicester, LE7 7FU, England.
Tel: (00 44) **0116 236 4325**
Fax: (00 44) **0116 234 0205**